For the Love of Blood 3

Lock Down Publications and Ca$h
Presents

For the Love of Blood 3

A Novel by *Jamel Mitchell*

For the Love of Blood

Lock Down Publications
Po Box 944
Stockbridge, Ga 30281

Visit our website @
www.lockdownpublications.com

Copyright 2023 by Jamel Mitchell
For the Love of Blood 3

First Edition May 2023
Printed in the United States of America

Lock Down Publications
Like our page on Facebook: Lock Down Publications @
www.facebook.com/lockdownpublications.ldp
Book interior design by: **Shawn Walker**
Edited by: **Kiera Northington**

Stay Connected with Us!

Text **LOCKDOWN** to 22828 to stay up-to-date with new releases, sneak peaks, contests and more…
Thank you.

Submission Guideline.

Submit the first three chapters of your completed manuscript to ldpsubmissions@gmail.com, subject line: Your book's title. The manuscript must be in a .doc file and sent as an attachment. Document should be in Times New Roman, double spaced and in size 12 font. Also, provide your synopsis and full contact information. If sending multiple submissions, they must each be in a separate email.

Have a story but no way to send it electronically? You can still submit to LDP/Ca$h Presents. Send in the first three chapters, written or typed, of your completed manuscript to:

LDP: Submissions Dept
Po Box 944
Stockbridge, Ga 30281

DO NOT send original manuscript. Must be a duplicate.

Provide your synopsis and a cover letter containing your full contact information.

Thanks for considering LDP and Ca$h Presents.

Jamel Mitchell

Chapter One

"Kill or be killed," Stacks stated.

"You right," Piru replied and fired his gun into his superior's chest. Santana and Simfany followed suit and emptied their clips. Simfany pulled another magazine from her waist and reloaded her gun. Santana put his hand across his mother's chest to stop her from firing again. They stood and watched as the blood ran down Stack's face, or what was left of his face.

"Come on, blood." Piru pulled Santana's arm. Piru went to grab Simfany also, but the gun in his face made all movement stop.

"What are you doing?" Piru looked into the barrel of Simfany's gun.

"That's where I know you from. I know I remembered your face." She smiled. "Almost, baby, almost." Santana watched from the side. He was fucked up over what was taking place, but his loyalty was forever with his mother. Santana shrugged out of Piru's grip and raised his gun.

"Ma, what the fuck is you talking about? This my man we got our guns trained on. I need to know what is going on." Santana looked back and forth between the two.

"Well, ask ya man why I got my fucking gun trained on his bitch ass. *Tell him or I will.* I thought I was tripping. Tell him, Patrick Mayfield. That is your real name. Tell him about the night you came to my doorstep them years before to pay me a visit. Who was it for? Stacks already admitted to the shooting. So why kill him? Why not let one of us end his career?" she asked Piru. All he could do was laugh.

"So you think shit funny. Well, let me tell you what I think I might have so far. I don't remember the face of the person who tried to kill me. I always remember the name though. I also remembered the voice of the person that pulled the trigger!" Simfany explained.

"What is she talking 'bout, nigga?" Santana gritted his teeth. His grip tightened on the trigger. Yet Piru said nothing. "How do you know this nigga was part of you being shot?" Santana asked Simfany.

"Because of the way he said Stack's name. It was the same way he said it the night I let him in our home on Edmonson. He gave me no chance to react to him. He opened fire and dropped his trademark on me, just like he did to Blaze and Ms. Harris. The only difference is I survived. And you, my baby, stayed in this fucked up ass state to seek revenge for the love of your raise." Simfany never took her eyes off of Piru.

"Ma, regardless, I'm riding with you but this shit not making sense. Stacks just said he was the one who shot you." Santana was confused.

"Nah, see, that's where you're wrong. He said that he knew I got shot and he was responsible. You still with me?"

"Yeah," Santana replied.

"A'ight. Stacks' bitch ass died with honor. He knew about the shooting hundred percent. What he didn't know was the shooter he sent to body me used his name. I'm thinking this was a small secret kept in between friends because I wouldn't be safe if all these reckless ass niggas would have known. Nigga, use your motherfucking head. Why you think Stacks looked at Piru and said 'Kill or be Killed'? It was a situation of *kill or be killed*." Piru raised his gun, showing his disloyalty. Why die alone? He wasn't about to, and this nigga here sensed that. So he killed the only thing to connect him to the shooting. We would have been sleeping with the enemy for real. It wouldn't surprise me if we found out he knew Jimdog. The only thing that fucked him up was you. He wasn't expecting to like you, so that killer in him made him recognize the real you possessed. He genuinely liked you, I can say that with truth. I was one of his missions. But regardless, he still tried to kill me." Piru just looked at Santana. Santana stared. Piru wouldn't reply.

"To make it easier, call your girlfriend. Ask her if Piru and Jimdog knew each other."

Santana looked at Piru for answers. He knew regardless of the outcome, whether his mother was right or wrong, Piru had to die. Santana knew Piru's pedigree. He was too dangerous to let live. He didn't want to be forced to watch his back again. Just food for thought, Santana pulled his phone out and placed the call to Paris. Unfortunately, her phone went straight to voicemail.

"Simfany, look, you tripping. I never been nothing but loyal to you and your son. I don't breed disloyalty. I could have killed you or your son. I was with the nigga all day, every day. It seems like I'm still about to die." Piru laughed at the karma that stared down the barrel at him. He turned to Santana.

"Shorty, know and understand you can't let your mother lead your life forever. To be there is fine because you know I believe loyalty is key, but to keep letting her run around paranoid killing shit with them crazy ass theories is wild. Regardless of the outcome, I love you, my nigga. Don't let her do this to all the niggas you grow to love!" Piru stated, knowing he couldn't escape his fate no matter what he said. "Do ya thing, shorty. I see you in hell."

Piru reached for his gun. Santana opened fire, the first slug opened Piru's face, ending his life immediately. The sirens in the distance and Simfany's yelling brought Santana out of his momentary daze. He had so much love for Piru that it broke his heart to be the one to end his life.

Simfany pulled at Santana's sleeve. He pulled away and walked to Piru's lifeless body. He lifted his gun again and fired two more shots into his head to confirm the kill. Ironically, Piru was the one who taught him to take precautions any time he pulled his trigger. He learned a lot from Piru. He would forever remember him. He turned to his mother. The look told him all. She felt like shit.

"Ma, this ain't the time to feel some type of way. We gotta get the fuck out of this bitch. Come on." This time he pulled her toward the door. She snapped out of her own trance and ran to her truck with Santana in tow. She hopped in the car and sped off, starting yet another war.

***

Hood Ru pulled into the complex only to be met by yellow tape and coroners. The police were everywhere. *What the fuck happened?* Hood thought as he backed up to leave. He was confused. He couldn't see what was going on because of the situation they had with the police officer only hours earlier. Hood didn't know if the officer died or not; he wouldn't find out now, that was for sure. Hood ducked low and sped down Trimble Road.

"Fuck, fuck, fuck!" He cursed himself. He tried to calm down. He fumbled for his phone. He dialed Piru's number from memory. The phone just rang. The voicemail picked up. He called back and again the voicemail picked up. *Man, fuck is this nigga at?* he thought angrily. He tried one more time, only coming up with the same outcome. Hood threw the phone into the divider and drove down Trimble Road until he got to the Joppatowne sector of the county.

Hood's safe haven was tucked off in Joppatowne. It was unknown to all but Stacks. Stacks knew everything about Hood. Their level of loyalty was never in question. He knew he was safe there. He parked his cherry red Caprice in the back of his home. He sat in the car and thought about what could be going on. Hood picked up his phone and called his best friend. For some odd reason, he knew Stacks wouldn't be able to answer either. The coroner's van told him a lot. He just didn't know who the bodies belonged to. He silently prayed to Allah, hoping that it wasn't any of his comrades that met their fate. Hood tried to clear his mind. He picked the phone off his lap and made another call, this time to Santana, his youngest goon. The phone rang for a while, but was answered.

"Yeah, what's poppin, my nigga? " Santana acted as if nothing was wrong.

"Where you at, ock?" Hood asked curiously.

"Hiding, hoping that detective nigga ain't dead. They already on my back for a body I didn't commit. Why? What's up? You good?"

"Yeah, I'm *hundred*. Is Piru still with you?"

"Nah, I left Ru and Stacks at the spot like two hours ago. That nigga Piru was supposed to be here like thirty minutes ago. The last time I talked to that nigga, I was leaving my raise. You know she still dizzy over the murder bullshit. Let that nigga Ru know he on some fuck shit for standing me up. Every second is critical, you feel me, son. You straight, though?" Santana asked.

"Not really. You ever feel like something was wrong? That's how I'm feeling right now. I just can't put my finger on it. What did them niggas say when you was leaving?"

"They were just chilling blowing that shit Piru copped. Nigga, there's something you not telling me. What is it?" Hood didn't know if he wanted to spill the news just yet. He knew if Piru was one of the bodies, Santana would go crazy. So he told him what he thought he should know.

"The police had the spot swarmed when I went over there. I didn't see anybody laid out on the curb waiting on the patty wagon, so they should be good. But until I get a call, that shit in the air." Hood told the partial truth. He didn't need Santana to start wilding out. He needed his youngin' to chill, especially if he might be the last of the dying breed. Literally.

"A'ight, my nigga. "I'm gone wait on Ru. If he calls, I'll call you. Keep me posted though, my nigga. I love you, homie!" Santana replied.

"All the time, ock, you know what is forever. Loyalty is everything. Be safe and call me if you hear anything."

"Stay 050"

"More less." The pair hung the phone up simultaneously. Hood smiled. His mind was fucking with him about his lost comrades. He had no hope no more. A part of him knew that his family met their ultimate fate. It was almost unheard of for a team like his to have the longevity that they experienced together. Hood knew what it was but he wanted to stay optimistic. Hood got out of his car and walked up to his door. He opened the many locks to his domain. Hood closed the

door behind him, only to be met face-to-face with the barrel of Santana's Glock. There was nothing more that needed to be said. Santana pulled the trigger, killing the last piece of his chess board. He hated it came down to ending all the lives of the niggas he grew to care for. But it was necessary if he wanted to live. Santana searched Hood's pocket for his phone. He couldn't leave any evidence of talking to Hood before he died. Santana shook his head as he dropped a red bandana on Hood's face.

"Blood in peace, my G," Santana stated before he stepped over Hood's body.

Jamel Mitchell

Chapter Two

Simfany just sat silently across from Santana. She didn't know what to say. She never thought Santana would kill Piru. Simfany had to admit one thing, Piru loved Santana like a little brother, but as she stated in the house, that didn't make it okay because he pulled the trigger trying to end her life. She was content with what happened. The only thing that bothered her was her son. He was lost. She could tell that the bodies were fucking with his head.

"Talk to me, Santana."

"What do you want me to say? I will always take your side over all. It's me and you till my dying date. There is nothing else to explain. I got you. Fuck them niggas, they dead now."

Simfany could hear the hurt in his voice.

"If it's worth anything, I'm sorry for dragging you into this." Santana turned around and looked at his mother.

"Excuse my language, but you're my mother—not my bitch. I will always ride for you, whether you're right or wrong. If you tell me to make the sky bleed, then that's what it is. So, chill, we're good. Please I mean that, ma. Can we go now?"

"What about Kevin and Tez-mo?" Simfany asked.

"They won't think twice about them niggas. They will ride if they find out, but they won't because we not going nowhere. We gone stay here and look these niggas in their eyes every day." Santana laughed but was deadly serious. He had no intentions of leaving the state.

"Now you're tripping. They are trying to get you for that murder earlier in the city. You got to leave until they figure out that you didn't do the shit," Simfany said.

"I'm just gone turn myself in. I was with . . ." He stopped midsentence. He burst out laughing. It was an eerie laugh. It sent chills down Simfany's back.

"What's so funny, boy?" she asked.

"All the niggas that can give me an alibi is dead. It's crazy, that's all!" Santana explained. "So what are we gone do?" Santana asked.

"Baby, the only place I can think of sending you back to is the city. But I'm pretty sure you will be looked for there. It's the only option though. Unless you got a better one." The look on Santana's face told her he didn't. Simfany walked over to her son and embraced him. She couldn't imagine what he could be going through. He laid his head on her chest like he always used to do as a kid.

"I love you, Santana. You don't ever forget that. I know most families shouldn't be going through this kind of struggle, but it was the cards we were dealt. I played a part in a lot of this fucked up cycle, but not on purpose. It's like I'm a trouble magnet. Thank you for being in my corner. That means a lot to me. Your dad would be proud of the type of person you are becoming." Santana just listened. The love was mutual; he expressed it a million times over and over. He enjoyed the comfort of being held by his mother.

"We'll figure something out before—" She was cut off by the buzz of Santana's ringtone. They looked at each other.

"Are you going to answer that?" Santana reached into his pocket and pulled out his phone. He looked at the incoming number. It was Tez-mo. He didn't want to answer the phone but he knew he had to.

"What's poppin, my nigga?"

"Ru, everything bad, shorty!" Tez-mo yelled through the receiver.

"Slow down, my nigga, talk to me. What you talking about?"

"Those hardback niggas killed Stacks and Piru, and we can't find Hood!" Tez-mo said frantically.

"Where you at, homie?" Santana could hear Kevin in the background going off on the police.

"I'm in the Commons. They got my niggas laid out on the ground in black bags. That shit crazy, Ru. I'm gone kill them niggas, shorty!" Tez-mo stated. "Hold on—Kev, chill, nigga!"

"Tell Kev to chill and stop acting off his emotions. That shit is dangerous. When Hood come around, tell him to call me. Keep ya head up, my G."

"You already know, West side shorty."

"All the time." Santana hung the phone up and put his cell phone back into his pocket.

Simfany looked at Santana for answers.

"What did he say?" Simfany asked.

"He called me to tell me that Stacks and Piru were killed by some Crip niggas." Simfany sighed.

"What did he say about Hood?"

"That he's basically missing, so right now we don't have to worry about nobody. They seem preoccupied. I gotta see what's going on with this other shit they trying to pin on me."

"We'll figure something out, baby boy."

"I know, ma. I know."

***

Detective Lawson stirred as he was being put into the helicopter.

"Sir, please don't move," the paramedic worker instructed. Blood ran down his midsection. Lawson was in a daze; he didn't understand what was going on.

"What—happ—to me?" he tried to ask but the oxygen mask constricted a lot of movements.

"Sir, please just be calm and stay still," the paramedic said as she held the gauze over one of his wounds. The noise from the helicopter nerved Lawson. He remembered scenes of what happened when he closed his eyes. He had been in plenty of gun fights but never outnumbered like he was earlier. He was hurting all over. His mind was numb.

"There are four entry wounds, one entry right cheek, one exit back side left ear, two wounds to the right upper chest cavity, and one wound bottom left abdomen." Lawson faded in and out as the paramedic looked over his body.

"Any internal bleeding?" the head medic asked.

"Not that I can see, sir." Lawson just laid still as the paramedics did their job. He was grateful for being alive. But his health was the last thing on his mind. He wanted revenge. Lawson was pissed for trying to do a good deed for a known criminal. Santana would have to figure out how to handle the murder on his own. He wasn't sure but he was almost sure enough to swear that Santana fired on him too. He would never forget the feeling of being gunned down. Lawson was thankful he wore his vest, but the pressure was just so intense. However, his vest didn't stop any of the bullets from piercing his skin.

"Sir, what is your name?" The paramedic asked.

"Detec—Laws—" he tried to respond. The look on the assistant medic's face grew fearful.

"Call the State Police. We have a detective shot badly. Call someone to inform them of this incident. Shit! What the heck is going on today?" Lawson closed his eyes and opened them back up. He wasn't dreaming; he really was fucked up. He was suffering from life-threatening wounds to his body and face. He didn't understand the severity of his condition. A calmness overtook his body as he lay still.

"Tree Top. . ." He smiled calmly as a tear rolled down his cheek.

"Excuse me, sir, what do you mean?" the paramedic asked. Lawson closed his eyes.

The helicopter was landing at Johns Hopkins Hospital when the detective's body began to go into violent spasms. The detective was pronounced dead twenty minutes later. The paramedics didn't know what to make of it, so they discarded his last statement. The Vasquez and Parks case died with Detective Lawson. The streets of Harford County had a more serious problem on their hands.

***

The death of Detective Lawson pulled national attention for help to catch his killers. What the news and the rest of America didn't know was: two of his killers were also dead and gone. Santana stayed off the streets and out of the way. The streets were on fire over the deaths of the TTP members. Hood Ru's body was found a week after his murder. After the remaining Tree Top members mourned the death of their fallen comrades, they took to the streets in a hail of gunfire. Each county felt the wrath of the gang's anger, as they literally painted the city red.

Chapter Three

"Santana!" Simfany called out. "Santana!" Simfany called out again. She still got no answer. Simfany feared the worst. She ran throughout the house looking for Santana. She ran to the only bedroom they had; they shared it. After the investigation began, she moved out of Meadowood and into a single-bedroom apartment in Baltimore County. They wanted to stay away from any place that would bring unwanted attention to them.

As she ran into the bedroom, she saw the gun trained at her. She ducked instinctively.

"Boy, what the fuck are you thinking?" Simfany yelled at Santana.

"I didn't know who was running in here," Santana replied as he put his gun back on the nightstand.

"I yelled ya name twice. How could you not hear me?" He just looked at her with a dumbfounded look on his face. She sucked her teeth and continued. "Anyway, I think I got somewhere you can go. You can live down there until we figure out something to do about this bogus ass murder charge." Simfany smiled.

"And where is this place you think you're about to send me to?" Santana asked curiously. "And who the fuck do you know down there?"

"First off, watch your mouth. *West Virginia*. You will be going down there with Lonnie's sister—Kat."

"You talking 'bout bad ass Kat?"

"Shut up, boy, yeah."

"I can feel that. She got like ten kids though."

"I know, but damn, it's better than being only half a county away from a life sentence. So pack whatever you want to take with you and get ready," Simfany said before she left the room. He sat up and stretched. Santana wanted to go somewhere but not to the west side of no damn Virginia. He really had no choice. He'd rather be there than stuck in somebody's jail fighting for his freedom. Simfany walked back into the room carrying a duffle bag. She sat next to him.

"What's that?" he asked.

"You will need money to survive, right? Okay then. Here, take this. You shouldn't have to ask for nothing. You're moving into a house with a lot of mouths to feed. When you get down there, you say nothing about your situation. If they ask, you just wanted to get out of the city for a while—" Santana cut his mother off.

"Why you keep using 'You' statements? You're sending me down there by myself?" Santana asked the obvious question.

"Yeah, you gotta leave. I'm gone be here to see what's going on. I'll be okay, trust me. You should know that. You're not the only one of us that can and will take someone's life to survive. I promise to remain safe. But right now getting you out of the state is my main objective."

"I can feel that. I'm still not feeling this though."

"You'll be okay, Santana. You got everything you need to live on ya own for a while." Simfany reached into the bag and pulled out a band of money. She handed it to Santana.

"What is this?"

"It's five thousand to get you on ya feet. You have to learn how to live on ya own for a while, baby boy. If you need anything, I'm only a phone call away. Oh, I almost forgot. Tijuana brought you a new phone as a going-away present, I guess."

"Did you tell her where I was going?"

"That's solely up to you. If you trust her enough with that kind of information, then you do you. This is where you use your own judgment. Don't get me wrong. I love Tijuana but there's just something you have to keep to yourself. But again you did a lot of time around her."

"I can respect it. But before I leave I want to see her. I got to write Drew a letter also. I haven't written him since I been home. Were you planning to drive me down there? How long is that going to take? Is the house big enough?" Santana shot each question out rapidly.

"Little boy, if you don't stop asking me so many questions, I'm gone beat ya ass up myself!" she joked. "I'll call her and ask her to come see me. She doesn't have to know anything about you being here."

"That's cool with me." Santana reached into the nightstand and grabbed a pen and paper. He had a lot to get off his chest. It was way past due. He drowned the rest of the world out and went to work.

***

Tijuana pulled into the apartment's drive way. She hadn't seen Simfany in a minute. She didn't know what to do after the kiss between her and Santana. She felt weird. Tijuana knew she had feelings for Santana, but the feelings didn't seem mutual and she understood that much. She told herself she did at least.

When she cut her car off, Simfany was waiting for her in the door way. The look on Simfany's face struck her as strange. She couldn't explain the look. She brushed it off for now. If it was something Simfany wanted to talk about, it would be brought up. She was glad to see Simfany. Tijuana knew Santana was on the run for the murder of Jimdog. She wished she could have seen him one more time before he left. She didn't understand why she couldn't shake her feelings for him. *That's a real ass lor nigga.* She smiled at the thought. She exited the car.

"What's up, baby girl? Long time no see!" Simfany ran into her arms.

"I miss you, ma," Simfany said excitedly.

"Bitch, I missed you too," Tijuana replied as they embraced.

"Come on, it's a lor chilly out here. How Tana holding up?" she asked.

"He doing okay, still crazy as ever. He misses you. Shit, at times he acts like he misses you more than he misses his raise." That statement made Tijuana smile big.

"What the hell does 'his raise' mean?" Tijuana had to ask. Simfany always says the word when it comes to Santana.

"I'm his raise. His mother."

"Oh. Duh. That's crazy. I didn't think of that. But what you been doing? I know it feels strange with Santana being gone again, huh?" Tijuana asked as they made their way into the home.

"So how you been holding up? It's been a long time since we talked about our lives."

"I been hold—" Tijuana stopped in her tracks. She covered her mouth in surprise and began to cry when she saw Santana on the stairs waiting for her arrival. Santana got up and walked over to Tijuana.

"Oh my Go—"

"Shhhh! I'm here, ma. I stayed just to see you before I left. Wipe ya eyes. I don't deserve them tears you continue to shed for me. How you been though, ma?" Santana asked as he held Tijuana in his arms.

"I'm good now, baby daddy." Everybody burst out laughing, causing the tension to disappear.

"Shut up, T, you a fool. I missed you though. That's crazy how you left niggas on stuck for like a month."

"I know I—." Tijuana tried to explain but was cut off.

"No need to explain to me. Everybody needs their own time. Regardless, you're loved over here. Thank you for the phone too."

"What phone?" Tijuana asked.

"The Sidekick you bought him a week ago," Simfany cut in.

"Oh yeah, you're welcome." She looked at Simfany and winked at her.

"Y'all niggas are fools," Santana said. They acted like he didn't see the wink. He shook his head.

"I'm gone give you two some time to talk," Simfany said as she grabbed her sweater and left the house. Tijuana looked at Santana. A new set of tears started to run down her face.

"Why do you keep crying, ma? I'm good, I promise. I didn't kill that nigga Jimdog. I'll be okay." Santana stammered, trying to explain.

"That's not what got me so fucked up. I love you, Santana, but I know it can never be. I watched you grow into a man. I'm proud of you. I know you 'bout to be gone for a minute but when you do come back I want you to give your girl a try," Tijuana said as she wiped her tears off her cheek.

"Why wait for your chance, ma? I may be in a fucked up situation but I'm good. After that night you kissed me and ran, I been fucked up. I've always loved you. I just didn't want to lose you as a friend. I rather we be cool till my body turn cold, than to start beefing over relationship issues. You feel me?"

"I can understand that."

"But like I said, we don't have to wait." Santana walked over to Tijuana.

"I love you, Santana," she said seductively.

"I love you too, beautiful." Tijuana grabbed Santana and pulled her into his arms. They looked each other in the eyes. Tijuana's eyes watered.

"Baby, stop crying, we here together," Santana assured.

"I know but I'm scared to lose you again. You don't understand, Tana. I really—"

"No need to explain, I know." Santana wiped the lone tear from her eye.

"Thank you." Santana silenced her with his own lips. He leaned in and kissed Tijuana. They kissed each other passionately. Santana pulled away from Tijuana.

"What's wrong?" Tijuana looked at Santana confusingly.

"Nothing. I just want to make sure this is what you want."

"Well, yes, this is what I want. But I know this don't stop here. We are one if you enter me."

"Say no more." He grabbed Tijuana's hand and pulled her into him. He kissed her before he lifted his own shirt over his head.

"Graveyard love," Tijuana whispered.

"Siempre," he replied in his native tongue. Santana broke the kiss again, this time to lead Tijuana upstairs to his bedroom.

By the time they made it upstairs, they both heard the door slam. Just to take precaution, Santana walked backed into the hallway to make sure it was his mother.

"Ma,"

"Yeah?"

"Nothing. I just wanted to make sure it was you." He didn't wait for her answer; he walked back into the room to a naked Tijuana. He closed the door and flipped the lock.

"So that's what it is?" he smiled.

"I'm all yours, Santana." Santana liked how that sounded. He laid Tijuana down on the bed and looked at her one more time.

"I dreamed many nights of having this opportunity. I love you to the core of your soul."

"I love you too, baby daddy," Tijuana said as she rubbed her hands through his hair. Tijuana sighed as Santana entered her. The look in both of their eyes said all that needed to be said. Santana leaned into Tijuana, bringing them together forever.

***

Simfany walked into the kitchen to put the food she brought away. Tijuana was missing in action. She already knew what time it was when she came in and Santana had no shirt on. Tijuana's moans only confirmed what she already knew. Simfany smiled as she made her way into the spacious living room. She took a seat on the couch and flicked through the channels until she found something she liked. She reached across the table and grabbed her purse. Simfany looked inside; she took the Glock 26 out to see the other contents. She grabbed the Dutch box of cigars. That was where she kept her own pre-rolled blunts. She opened the box and took out two blunts and sat them to the side. Simfany put everything back into the bag except her gun. It was just a calm feeling when she had her life in her control, and that's what the gun that sat on the coffee table made her feel like. She lit the first blunt and blew it to the face.

Simfany sat and looked back on the life she led for herself and Santana. Never in a million years could somebody tell her that her life would end up this complicated. The weird thing was, she liked how her life turned out. She was blessed. She had a son that adored her, and enough money to live a comfortable life. The move to Baltimore was a bad one. That one decision left a lot of lost souls in her path. Even though she would never know, but that move out of New York affected a lot of people's lives, especially Justice's and Lonnie's. Simfany knew she had to let her heart grow cold to survive. Believe it, she was cool with that. Piru's last words haunted her most. She would never forget when he looked back at Santana and told him, "Don't let her kill all the niggas you grow to love." *Why do I keep thinking about that shit?* she asked herself. It fucked her up, but she knew the truth. Fuck that nigga. *Goonz get burnt too,* she laughed at her own humor. Simfany pulled on the Dutch Master and drifted into a world she knew all too well.

***

Santana looked into Tijuana's eyes as they lay there.

"What?" she asked.

"Nothing, just admiring your beauty." He kissed her forehead.

"Thank you."

"What you thanking me for?"

"Everything. You been *hundred* since the first day I seen you inside the gym on Clinton. I would never think it would've come to this, but I'm happy for the first time since my brother passed away. So thank you."

"You're welcome, ma, but I don't deserve any credit. You chose me when I was only a young nigga. All the praise is due to that nigga upstairs. It was a hard road but he brought you into my life. My nigga, you kept it *hundred* too. Give yaself some credit!" Santana replied as he looked into her eyes.

"Stop doing that. You're driving me crazy. I can still feel you inside of me," Tijuana said seductively. Santana grabbed her waist and pulled her closer to him. "You better stop. Ya mom's gone kill us." They both laughed.

"Shit, she the one running around here playing match maker. She ain't slick."

"But on a more serious note where does this leave us now?" Tijuana asked.

"I'm with whatever, ma. Because I know it will never be the same again. I've loved you forever. Are you ready to fuck with a nigga of my caliber though?"

Tijuana laughed.

"What's that supposed to mean, Mr. Caliber? You stupid, but I want you to be mine and only mine," Tijuana said, meaning every word.

"You sure you want to fuck with a nigga that's on the run for murder?"

"We'll go one day at a time, baby daddy." She laughed.

"I'm for real, Tijuana. I'm not trying to commit to some bullshit. I'm not trying to fall in love with you and you leave when shit gets rough."

"Siempre, right?" Tijuana asked.

"Siempre," Santana repeated as Tijuana licked down his body, taking him into her mouth.

Chapter Four

Santana sat at the edge of the bed trying to gather his thoughts, while Tijuana lay still. He knew that what he and Tijuana had wouldn't be able to actually work. It was crazy he even got the chance to live out the vision.

Tijuana stirred.

Santana turned and looked at Tijuana; he admired her beauty. He could see himself being with shorty forever. Tijuana peaked out from under the cover. That made him smile.

"What you looking at, lor nigga?" she said playfully as she yawned.

"I don't want no beef, ma."

"You better not!" Tijuana said, stomach full of butterflies.

"Oh yeah." Santana quickly spun and crawled up the bed.

"Baby, stop!" Tijuana screamed as she tried to hide under the covers. The attempt was feeble.

"Good morning, beautiful," Santana whispered into her ear.

"Awwwww." She pulled the covers from over her head. Santana leaned in and kissed her soft lips.

"Thank you, baby daddy."

"My pleasure, ma."

"Santana, we really need to talk. I know we already talked about this, but lust was involved. So we need to talk about this on different terms. I'll give you what I got, or do you want to go first?" she asked

"Do your thing," he stated and gave her his undivided attention.

"Alright. I really love you, Santana, and even though you're young as hell, I see more in you than I see in these lame-ass niggas my age or maybe even older. I have a lot of respect for you. Let me just put it this way, you're the type of nigga that I want my children to grow up idolizing. I know shit you're into now isn't what I want for my children, but I beg every night that he gives me a child that's as loyal as you. I want badly to be cherished like you cherish Simfany. I admire
the fuck out of you for that. I will be here for you forever if you let me." The laugh Santana produced while she was talking embarrassed

her.

"Why are you laughing, Santana?" she asked in a low whisper. He could tell he hurt her feelings. Tijuana recoiled back under the cover. She was on the verge of tears.

"Ma, I'm laughing because—look, ma, I never lied to you before, so I won't now. That's what was running through my mind as I sat at the edge of the bed. I can't see this working, I mean honestly. Imagine this, when I do get locked up for that murder hanging over my head, where would that leave us? Time will change everything!" Santana explained.

"Nah, fuck that shit!" Tijuana came from under the covers with tears streaking down her cheeks. "Nigga, I love you and I swear on Kane's grave I'll go through any and everything with you. That murder charge means nothing to me, nigga. If you're scared to commit, then say so, save all that extra shit for the birds. So with that being said, are we going to try and make this work or not. Loyalty is everything, right? Baby, I got you, don't continue to push me away. Please. I'm not asking for much." Santana looked Tijuana in her eyes, the stains of her tears still visible. He was lost for words. He knew what he wanted and he knew what it was. The time away was the distracting part. He was so lost in his thought he didn't give her an answer.

"Santana, say something." She sat up, letting the covers fall to her waist, showing her bare breasts.

"Santana!"

"I know, ma, please for a second just listen and hear me out. Let me speak my peace."

"I'm all ears." Her face showed fear of the unknown.

"Tijuana, it's no secret I have a lot of love for you, I have since I first met you. This murder bid hanging over my head is making me doubt not only you, but myself. I wanna be *hundred* with you. You are everything I'm looking for in a female. I just don't know if we as a couple are ready."

"But Santa—"

"Let me finish, ma. What I'm saying is I'm willing to try. I know you're different, but I feel like this still needs to be said. Tijuana, don't do me dirty, not now, not later, not never. If we're going to be one, then that's what it is. I just ask for your loyalty. You never had a problem giving me that before, so I expect the same love. Don't change."

"What about your girlfriend Paris?'

"Let me deal with that. I can't fuck with shorty. Once I found out that Jimdog was the father of her child, it was too much for me." He explained, telling half of his truth. If he didn't have the murder charge hanging over his head, he knew Paris would be his shorty. He tried to act and play as if he didn't have love for Paris no more, but in truth, it was just the opposite. The only thing that stopped him from being with Paris is Jimdog. Knowing this, he kept it to himself; Tijuana didn't need to know that. Deep down he knew they weren't good for each other, but he couldn't figure out why. One thing he believed religiously was, everything happened for a reason. Everything was predestined. He learned quickly how to play his cards as they were dealt. Tijuana was the queen of his deck. He was ready to play spades deck face up.

"Say no more. I'll leave all the worries to my king." Santana smiled. It was crazy like she read his mind. He was just going to put his faith in God to protect him from evil.

"Don't worry about nothing, ma, if it's meant to be, Allah will make sure we good. Just have faith and remain loyal. If you never fold on my terms, forever we will stand. Right now the obstacles we face are these charges and me going *OT*–out of town."

"I'm coming with you," Tijuana said firmly. Santana smiled.

"I have no problem with that. I'm not planning to run forever. I'm not trying to set roots on the west side of Virginia. You feel me?"

"I understand but we need each other now more than ever. Please don't leave me by myself again." The look on her face was that of sincere love.

"Look—" He sighed. "Let me get settled and I promise to send for you. I wanna make sure it's a good place to be first. I rather live with you than with one of my mother's friends anyway. Just be patient. You cool with that?" Santana asked.

"I have no choice. I love you, Santana

"I love you too, beautiful. My word: it'll work, all it takes is dedication and loyalty. We'll be good until our souls touch the sky."

"I wish my brother was here. I know he would have loved you. You're heaven-sent, baby. I thank whoever made this possible for us. I guess if that's on the soul of Jimdog so be it. Siempre!" Tijuana repeated what she always heard Santana and Simfany say.

"Forever, ma, forever." He crawled back into the bed with his queen. He knew he had to enjoy his freedom while he had the chance. It was possible at any moment it could change, whether it be a six by nine or an early grave. As they lay in each other's arms, a million thoughts ran through both Santana and Tijuana's head; and the two growing lives inside Tijuana wasn't one.

Chapter Five

Drew walked down the hall of Unit 1 (King Hall) as Tijuana came down the stairs from the top of the unit.

"Long time no see, shorty," Drew stated as he opened his arms to embrace Tijuana.

"Awwww, it sound like you miss someone," she replied.

"Maybe. What's good with Santana?" Tijuana's eyes lit up at the mention of Santana's name.

"What you all smiles about?" He laughed. He knew what it was, but let it be what it be.

"He's okay, I actually got a letter from him for you." She reached into her pocket and pulled out a single piece of paper. "I have to go, but if you write back give it to me and I'll make sure Santana gets it. Be discreet because you know he's on the run for that body in Baltimore a couple of weeks ago. I'm sure he explained enough. I love you, Drew. Be good."

"Love you too, sis, good looking." Tijuana leaned in and kissed her brother on his cheek. Tijuana turned to leave.

"T?" She stopped and turned around to the only other brother she had left.

"Take care of my nigga, shorty."

"I will. You just make it home and all will be well."

"I can do that."

Tijuana walked off leaving Drew in the back hall by himself with a letter from his right-hand man. Drew wasted no time and opened the letter. The letter didn't contain much to a regular person but it contained a lot to him. He read:

My G, ain't much I can say for the lost time, but never question loyalty. You know what it is. Things happen and bodies were dropped, putting me in a fucked up situation. Be patient, you're not forgotten about. I didn't do the letters when I was in there, so you know it will be harder out here to do so. But I love you, nigga, no homo. My mom sends her love. I'll be missing in action because of this body over my head. If I'm home or not when you get out, I'll make sure you're good. Win, lose, or draw, my G, you my brother.

Santana...

Just a few lines was enough to satisfy Drew, he understood what it was to let the streets grab a hold again. That night he went to sleep with a new sense of motivation.

***

Charleston, West Virginia. Simfany pulled onto Jackson Street on the city's East End. Santana looked at the homes that lined the blocks. It didn't look as country as he expected it to. Shit, he didn't know what to expect. Kat was on the porch waiting on their arrival.

"Hey, beautiful!" Kat called out, baby in arm. Simfany cut the car off as Santana exited the Tahoe.

"Hey, baby, I'm doing okay. How you been doing? When you going to stop popping them kids out?" Simfany laughed but was curious.

"Only the Lord knows." Kat smiled, showing the golds in her mouth. Santana stood there and looked at the ground. He was acting like a shy little boy. Kat was still the same as she was back in the day before they moved out of the city. Kat was still sexy as hell. Her Latin features demanded attention. Kat's look was extremely exotic. She resembled the likes of Shakira, but in all honesty she was colder than that. She was a sight you would only believe if you had seen it for yourself.

"Hey, Santana, I see you don't know no one anymore," Kat smirked at him. Santana looked up at her. Her hazel eyes were so beautiful, he got lost in them for a second or so.

"Nah, it ain't that, ma, I'm just a quiet person. But how could I ever forget you!" He let his last comment hang high.

"I know that's right. He not a child no more, Kat, you better watch yourself." Santana's face turned beet red from his mother's statement. Kat acted like she didn't hear Simfany.

"So what's up? Why you sending him down here? He been fucking up?" Kat asked.

"Nah, he ain't a bad kid. I just need a break, plus he was getting tired of Baltimore already. You know he just got out of juvey. I would have sent him to New York; you know Lonnie isn't fit to take care of him. You're the only person I trust. It'll only be until the end of the year. Is that cool with you?"

"That's cool," Kat replied. "What do you want me to do as far as school and shit?" Kat asked. The mother in her was on point. Simfany laughed.

"Ask him." Simfany poked her lips out and rolled her eyes. Santana chimed in.

"I was kicked out for assault," he explained while he looked into Kat's eyes.

"Dracula all day. The only difference between the two of you, Cartez had that NBA talent so they turned a blind eye to all the shit he did." Kat knew all too well. Kat was Melrose for real.

"I got him, Simfany."

"I know you do. Thank you. I would stay but I'm trying to beat the sun home." Simfany reached into her purse and pulled out some money wrapped in a rubber band. She tried to hand the money to Kat.

"Thank you but I'm okay. I'm doing this out of love for you and yours, ma. No money needed; if it's needed I'll contact you. All I ask is that he is okay financially. I do have a lot of mouths to feed." Kat explained as she pushed the money back into Simfany's palm.

"You sure, ma?" Simfany asked.

"Yeah, you chilling for the night?"

"Bitch, you been smoking that green. I told you I have to beat the sun home. Plus I don't want people to miss me too much." She winked at Kat.

"Drive safely, boo." Santana walked to the porch and waited for Kat and his mother to finish their conversation. *Damn, another city. How the fuck do I keep running myself in these situations.* Kat and Simfany walked up to Santana.

"Let me talk to my son really quick, ma," Simfany told Kat. Kat walked into the house, leaving the two to their privacy.

"Be good out here but you know what it is. Don't let none of these niggas act crazy. Shoot first, ask questions later. Please be safe. I'll be back soon. Whenever you need money just hit me and I got you. I love you, Santana. Please be careful." Santana looked away. His eyes began to water up. Simfany was Santana's only weakness. She wiped his tears away.

"I love you, baby," she said before she kissed him and walked off.

"I love you too, pretty lady. I promise to be safe. It's these niggas you have to worry about." He tried to make light of the situation.

"Stay out of trouble, Santana. You hear me?" Simfany said with a no-nonsense look on her face.

"Yes, ma'am. What's understood don't need to be explained. Love you, ma." He knew she wasn't playing, but she also knew if need be he wouldn't hesitate.

"Love you too, baby." Simfany backed away from the home on the corner of Jackson Street. Their relationship was like no other. They communicated through silence until she was inside her Tahoe. Before Simfany drove off, she blew Santana a kiss. Santana returned the gesture. He watched as the truck pulled off and drove down the block. He rubbed his hand through his hair and sighed.

"Boy, where your bags at?" Kat called from the door, breaking him from his current thought.

"I didn't bring nothing. My mom gave me money to buy some new things."

"Cool, come in. We have to talk a little." Kat moved to the side to let Santana into the house.

"So what's up?" Santana asked as he sat on the arm of the sofa.

"All I ask is that you don't get hurt or bring the police to my house. You're old enough, so please act like it. Not much but that's my rule."

"That's easy enough. If you need me for anything just ask and I got you. And I mean *anything*." He winked at her. Kat laughed.

"Boy, I see you going to be a handful."

"Where is Montez at?"

"At school with his bad ass. Raven and her little one in there though." Montez, Raven and Jasiah were the only kids that he knew from the hood. He remembered that Jasiah was the oldest of the three. Then it was Raven and Montez. Kat had two other children since she moved to West Virginia. Santana learned quickly that his mother was the baby out of Lonnie and Kat.

"I apologize but I'm tired from that long ass drive. What room am I in?" Santana asked.

"You and Montez sharing a room."

"Good looking, beautiful." That made Kat blush.

"Thank you for the compliment."

"Only truth, ma, now where is Montez's room?"

"Go up the stairs, make a left and it's the last room on the right," Kat explained.

"Thank you." Santana yawned and followed Kat's directions to the tee. Santana closed the door. He waited a couple of minutes before he took the Glock off his hip and placed it underneath the pillow he was about to lie on. He combed his hair into a ponytail and laid down; within minutes he was sleep. It was the only place he could ever find peace.

Santana was awakened to the shaking of his leg.

"Wake up, bruh." Santana opened his eyes, his head resting against the pillow where his gun also rested. Santana sighed; he knew he was caught dead to rights. Yet he reached under the pillow and gripped the Glock 27. If all fails, he knew for sure the 40. caliber shells from his Glock would eat whatever stood in its way. Santana turned his head; the dark-skinned nigga looking back at him was Montez's scared ass. Montez was happy to see him; Santana felt the same though, so he let the grip go on his gun and smiled.

"Damn, my nigga, it's been a long time," Santana said as he wiped the cold out of his eyes.

"Shit, bruh, like eight years. It's been a grip, that's for sure. So what sent you to the country? I heard you was in juvey the last I talk to the fam."

"I was, but I been home a little minute now. Just time for a change of scenery. Gotta chill for a minute. Niggas is getting wild back home!" Santana stated. He didn't want Montez to know much of his situation. Nowadays you never know what people's motives were.

"I bet you still flicked up over the shit with Peewee and lil' bruh. I know those was your niggas. I knew that blood shit lil' cuz was on was liable to get him or someone around him killed." Montez's playful tone grew serious when he talked about his cousin. Santana saw the love that lived in Montez for Justice.

"It's reality, my nigga. The niggas that you're willing to die for are usually the ones that take your life. And most of the times it's to the love of money, females or pure jealousy." The subject of being loyal touched Santana's heart every time. He was currently fighting his own demons dealing with the deaths of Piru and Hood Ru. Stacks was another story; he could care less about him. He was taught to play for keeps if he was going to play the game. One of his rules was to never let his emotions control his actions. Santana's thoughts were his only enemy at the moment. He had an angel to his right and a jinn to his left. It was a constant inner war against good and evil. Montez wasn't a killer or close to it, so he didn't understand or know what to say. Montez was lost for words, so he changed the subject.

"So, bruh, what you been doing with ya life?" Montez asked.

"A juvenile bid," he answered, telling only half the truth. The rest wasn't his business.

"I knew you was going to be the wild one. You used to trip on the kids in the big park all the time. Nigga Drac ya pops. That nigga was known for that loud bang, so it's only right that you are too. Like father like son." Montez laughed. "You smoke?"

"Occasionally," Santana answered as he stood and stretched.

"A'ight, give me a second. Raven always in here with her nosey ass. I gotta hide the middy from her!" Montez explained, leaving the room. Santana walked into the hallway looking for a bathroom. The bathroom was right beside Montez's room. Santana walked in and shut the door behind him and sighed. He looked into the mirror and saw his own features staring back at him, but he didn't recognize the person staring back at him. Santana turned on the water and washed his face. The sleep, the stress and his past slid down the drain as the water disappeared.

"Lil' bruh, you in there?" Montez called from the other side of the door.

"Yeah, here I come, my G," he replied back at Montez's annoying. He dried his face with the paper towels that was laid across the top of the toilet. He dropped the damp towels into the trash can. He looked in the mirror again before he left. Even though what he saw should have worried him, it didn't. Santana didn't care; he was content with what he saw. And at the end of the day that was all that mattered. He exited the bathroom and went back into Montez's room.

"My nigga, why is your—" Santana didn't see Raven at first but he heard her voice. His words stuck in his throat when he looked up and saw Raven. Damn, she cold-blooded, he thought as he looked at Raven in awe. She was sexier than her mother. She was prettier than he could last remember.

"Come here, boy!" Raven exclaimed. "You got all the sexy on me. Damn, Santana." That made Santana blush for sure. Montez laughed at the color of his beet red face. All Santana could say to Raven's compliment was:

"Likewise. You're also very beautiful."

"Chill, Raven, that nigga getting all red and shit," Montez continued to joke.

"Shut up with ya ugly ass. Don't pay him any attention with his good hating ass!" Raven teased.

"Thank you for the compliment," Montez said, flashing a smile. Her insult went in one ear and out the other.

"Y'all niggas crazy. I hear you're a mother now. First, congratulations. Secondly, where little momma at?"

"She's asleep, that little girl is the devil, I tell you. But I love my baby to death. She just bad as hell." Santana sat on the end of the bed.

"What's her name?" Santana asked, now looking up into Raven's seductive ass gaze.

"Niyah," she replied.

"That's cute."

"Thank you." Raven smiled big. Montez caught her gesture out the air.

"Raven, he said her name was cute, not you!" Montez joked.

"Shut the fuck up with your lame ass!" Raven exclaimed.

"Why you even in here? Get out."

"Talk to you later, Santana," Raven stated before she stormed out of the room, slamming the door behind her. *Damn, shorty crazy!* Santana thought to himself.

"Don't mind her, bruh, she always acting like a little slut."

"I know that's your fam, but let me say something. I don't care what she out there in them streets doing. Show her respect, especially in the presence of others. Real shit, my G."

"I can understand what you're saying but, my nigga, she be on that bullshit," Montez tried to explain.

"Listen, Montez, that's your blood, my nigga, respect her like so, because these niggas will see you disrespect her and they won't show no respect. Then if you the nigga I think you are, you'd bust their heads for disrespecting the home front. To avoid the jail time or bullshit now, give her your upmost. But that's solely on you to do. Pass that blunt through, damn nigga."

Santana had to speak his peace because if Kat let that nigga get away with it, then it occurs all the time. "Real niggas don't disrespect any females in their family. I don't care what part of the street they are involved in."

"I feel you, bruh," Montez said, brushing Santana off.

"A'ight, my nigga, food for thought." Montez took another hit from the rolled blunt before he passed it. Santana sat in silence as he thought about what type of nigga Montez turned into. The thoughts he held for Montez disappeared with the last pull of marijuana. He promised himself to not pay Montez any attention. Santana knew what kind of person Montez was: a fucking pot head! He couldn't use a nigga like that. So, at the moment, whether Montez knew it or not, Santana lost a lot of love for him and he became a pawn in his world.

They smoked the rest of the blunt and talked about the little things in the life they lived differently. Santana spoke about his time in Hickey. He wanted to let Montez know that it wasn't sweet in juvey. He didn't know about the system out here, but in Baltimore shit was real. Montez listened and told Santana about friends he hung out with. The person that stuck out most was the quiet get-money nigga Montez always talked about. If he wasn't mistaken, the nigga's name was Zachariah, or something close to it. Santana wanted to meet Zachariah.

All the people in Santana's life were either killed or left for dead. All he knew was pain. He wanted to turn a new leaf. His father was one of the biggest drug dealers his hood ever saw. Santana knew deep down he had that animal in him to get money. He knew his mother had money if he needed, but him being the man he grew into, he wanted to make a way for himself. He didn't want any more bodies on his head. So a change would need to take place. The only issue with that was, he was a killer through and through. At a young age Santana was taught to survive and protect, and that was all he knew. Change is hard, but he was willing to fall back and get money and leave all the bullshit behind. If he knew that these country ass niggas played for keeps, his mindset would have remained on its original state—kill or be killed.

Jamel Mitchell

Chapter Six

The streets of Charleston were definitely different from the streets of New York or Baltimore. As for the pros of the state, there were females everywhere. That was a plus coming from the situation that he just left. He actually had a chance to relax and think as a kid his age. Santana had stayed put to get to know his now second family. Raven was a precious soul, and her daughter Niyah was even more precious. He enjoyed them all except Montez; the boy was a cry baby. All he worried about was smoking his weed and the little bitches he chased on a daily basis. Santana was raised in a different environment, so he couldn't understand. Family values mattered more than anything. However, Montez choose his friends and the substances over his blood. Santana found that extremely weak. He let Montez do him though. He was only there for a couple of days so he didn't want to ruffle any feathers. He did his best to tolerate Montez and his situation; he let go and let God deal with it.

Santana walked down Jackson on his way to the corner store. The gas station that sat on Washington Street and Ruffner Avenue was the most frequently used store on the city's East End. The Shop n Go was jumping at all times of the day. Fiends were out, the drunks were posted trying to get a beer from everybody coming and going. The scene was that of a true city. It kind of fucked Santana up a little; he wasn't expecting this kind of country shit. When he thought of the country, he pictured niggas with golds and cars. He pictured homes and stores being far away from where he would live. He thought of just a way slower environment, but he was mistaken. The only difference was, the metro commute was different, but the city was here. He could see it. He wouldn't let these niggas fool him; he was too smart for that.

"What's up, lil' brother? How you doing? You got some spare change?" The drunk wobbled over to him as he made his way into the Shop n Go. Santana ignored the man and walked into the store. He hated to see people so fucked up. He promised himself everyday he couldn't turn out like that. He walked to the freezer and pulled out a beer, the same one the drunk was sipping on. He shook his head at the cold beverage. He then went to what he really came for—the notebook, pencils and pens. He needed to holla at his brother from another. Drew was about to come home soon. Santana wanted bro to be straight and he needed to drop a line; the letter was overdue. Santana grabbed a red, college-ruled pad and some red and blue pens. Santana walked up the front with the beer and writing utensils in hand; he sat them on the counter.

"Do you have ID on you to pay for that beer?" the clerk behind the counter asked.

"Nah, but it's not for me. I got it for—" Santana tried to explain before his statement was cut short.

"You might as well take that back to the freezer then, because you won't leave here with that." Santana laughed. The clerk was serious.

"Well, that's cool, but if you would have listened to me the first time when I tried to tell you what it was for, you would have understood a little better. I'm buying this for the drunk that's hanging out front of your spot. Don't worry. I won't take it nowhere. I'll pay for it and send the dude in here to get it. Is that cool with you, my nigga?" Santana explained without blinking an eye at clerk.

"My fault, little man. I just got this job. I'm just trying to keep it, that's all." The clerk rung up the items for him. "Anything else, bruh?"

"Yeah, let me get a box of them Honey Dutch Masters. I'll have him come and get that too. Also give me a book of stamps. That's all. Please give the man the change. Thank you." Santana sat a twenty dollar bill on the counter and grabbed the writing paper and the stamps and left. He tucked the pens in his pocket as he pushed the door open. The drunk was still out there harassing people for money. Santana shook his head at the sight. *Niggas is better than this*, he thought to himself. He waited for the person to pull off from the gas pump to holler for the drunk man. When the car pulled off, it left only them two at the gas pump.

"I left a beer in there and some money. Go in there and grab those blunts for me. Understand I didn't do it for cigars. I did it so you can stop asking people for shit. Get your shit together, my nigga. Show me around and I'll make sure you good. Go grab them cigars for me and holler at me." The drunk didn't say nothing back. He just turned and walked into the store and grabbed his beer, the cigars and the change.

"Thank you, lil' souljah," the drunk said.

"Are you from here?" Santana asked.

"No, I'm from New Orleans originally. I got caught up in a murder rap and my niggas left me down here by myself. I been down here for twenty plus years now. As you can see, I'm fucked up. This poison got me, you hear me?" the drunk said as he held up the 40.02 of Steele Reserve. Santana nodded.

"I understand, OG. Do you have a place to stay and shit like that?" Santana asked. Each word he spoke, the man seemed to sober up. The young kid had a lot of questions; he had to be on point with this one. The old head could see that. He stopped drinking and gave Santana his undivided attention.

"Yeah, I don't do this all the time. I needed a beer so I sat out here and asked a couple of people. I thank you too, lil' souljah."

"Do you know enough to show me around and tell me what's what?" Santana looked up into the eyes of the drunk.

"Yeah, I told you I been stuck down this muthafucka forever. What's your name, souljah?"

"Santana," he said with pride.

"That's your name or your government?"

"My real name. Why?"

"Just a question. You must be planning to stay for a while, because if you are then telling people your real name, it's okay, but if you're planning to do some hot shit—nicknames only. By the way, souljah, how old are you?"

"I just turned sixteen, but please don't let the age fool you. I haven't done much, but I've been through all and some." Santana wanted the old head to know he wasn't just another dancing young nigga. The pretty boy look threw a lot of people for a loop when shit got real.

"What you about to do right now, souljah?" the drunk asked.

"Go write one of my brothers I was in juvey with," Santana replied.

"That's what's up. Look, I live in the cut near Chamberlain Court. The houses right behind the Roosevelt Center. I'll be out there. Holla at me whenever you're ready to know about the history of the streets of Charleston. A lot of souls were lost to guns of the men of this city. The only advice I can give you right now is, don't take these niggas to be sweet. Their guns bust too, if not more. Just holla at me, soulja, I can see it in your eyes." The drunk walked off. His whole swag changed; he was no longer just the old drunk he saw only minutes before. Santana walked back home. The old drunk raised a lot of questions in his head. Santana could tell he might have been that nigga back in his day. *Though now he was washed up, old and drunk, this nigga looked me in my face and told me he could see it in my eyes, I saw all I needed to see in his*, he thought as he walked into his home on Jackson Street.

***

Simfany sat silently in the dark, as she watched Bogus squirm around trying to get out of the rope that had his hands and feet bound together. The metal chair that he was strategically placed in rattled at his every move. The knot tying lessons she took at the community center when she was a little girl came in handy after all. The look on Bogus' face after he woke up was priceless; the big gang banger was scared, maybe for the first time in his life. It gave Simfany a sense of power. It made her pussy wet.

"The more you move, the more you're going to squish the shit in your boxers around." Simfany laughed to herself as she rubbed a small portion of Vicks under her nose. The vapor rub didn't erase the smell completely but it eliminated most of it. One thing she had to admit: the nigga wasn't trying to tell her nothing, but she also hadn't begun to really torture him yet. She would find out what happened the night that her nephew was gunned down. Simfany needed to know the story behind his death. She got up and walked to the spot where Bogus was tied down.

The darkness only let Bogus see little, but his eyes were adjusted enough to see something coming at him. He tried to duck but without luck; the blade caught the flesh on his face and cut him deeply. For a minute he thought he escaped the blow until he felt the watery fluid running down his face. Simfany had sliced him with a box cutter. She opened his face wide open.

"Simf, I swear, ma, I wasn't responsible for what happened to your little man. That's on blood, ma, I swear. Please, shorty."

"Nigga, fuck you and that blood shit. Now what the fuck happened that night my baby was murdered? And I swear you better tell me soon. I know a bunch of hungry ass niggas that want ya head, blood!"

"I swear all I know is—" Bogus coughed. "I swear all I know is, Peewee was out for blood when he found out that Justice was fucking with Desi." He coughed badly from the blood that slowly tricked down his throat.

"You really think I'm playing with you, huh?" She pulled her Glock off her hip and pressed it to his knee cap and before he got the chance to move and protest, she squeezed the trigger twice, shattering both his knees in half.

"Aaaaaarrrrgghhhh!" Simfany smiled. That got his attention.

"Now tell me what the fuck I want to know. I know Destiny was the ultimate reason behind Peewee's disloyalty, but bitch, what part did you fucking play!" Before he could answer, she pressed the gun into his right thigh and squeezed the trigger, sending a bullet through his leg and lodging it into the floor of the old basement.

"That was just in case you thought I was playing. Now tell me what the fuck happened, Bogus. I promise I won't ask you no more." She pulled an army style knife out of her pocket. *If this nigga don't tell me what the fuck I need to know I'm going to cut every vein in his body*, she thought to herself as she looked him in his eyes. The clatter of his teeth began to annoy her.

"Bogus!"

"Alright, I used—when I tell you this, will you let me go?" Bogus asked, already knowing the answer.

"As a matter of fact I will. I promise. I put it on my slain love." Simfany waited for Bogus to speak, but he remained silent. The darkness is what kept him on his toes and scared to death. He wouldn't be able to see any attack that she would perform.

"Nigga, what's up? Talk. What the fuck you waiting on?" Simfany was growing impatient.

"Give me a second. I can barely breathe, ma." He shifted he weight, scrapping the metal chair across the floor. "Simfany, you know what's crazy? All this shit started with you being shot in Baltimore. I tried to get Justice to go down there for you and in my eyes he froze up." Bogus coughed hard; it almost sounded like he was gargling. Bogus continued. "And from that day forward it's been a battle between egos. I looked at it like this—if the roles were reversed, Santana wouldn't have hesitated, no matter what he was going through." Simfany smacked the shit out of Bogus.

"Nigga, shut the fuck up and tell me what I want to hear. All that other shit leads to this, yeah, but the fact that my little nigga was killed changes the game more than a little bit. So tell me what the fuck I want to hear." The clicking of her stilettos made Bogus's heart race. It was as if his heart was in tune with her heels, so when she stopped walking it felt like his heart would also stop. *To die right now wouldn't be so bad*, Bogus thought to himself. The room all of a sudden came to life, blinding both of them. The basement was empty besides the light that illuminated it and the two people in it. Simfany let her eyes adjust to the brightness of the light; she opened her eyes to a bloody Bogus. He had feces coming out of his boxers; his knees or what was left of them was disfigured. The man was flicked up. The gash in his face was the most vicious; the meat that hung from his jaw bone was white as a sheet. It stuck out even through heavy clots of blood. *At least I didn't beat his eyes to death*, she laughed at her ill humor. She was loving every minute of her torture game.

"So you going to tell me what I wanna know so I can leave or do you want me to use this handy blade of mine?" She pulled the army looking blade from behind her back. Bogus felt his heart sink into his stomach. The sight of the knife was enough to make him tell whatever he knew and why he knew it.

"Simf—Simfany, look. Here it is, when I saw Justice wondering down the block I called Peewee and told him to go get the gun so we could scare him." He coughed up blood and spit it out the best he could. The gash in his cheek played a big part in his breathing. He continued.

"My bad. Okay, I called Peewee and told him to grab the ratchet so we could scare Justice for being out after dark. He was all for the joke. I hadn't even been in the hood for a while. That was actually my first night back." He spit out another glob of blood, but this time his cough was much lighter.

"I had just come to the hood to shoot some dice with all the little homies. Not in a million years would I have thought that Justice would come up and start shooting with us. But he did and he started stinging us too. Things got out of hand like they always do." She caught his remark as soon as he said it and he would pay for it.

"Nigga, keep going before I stick this blade in your bitch ass." Simfany moved closer to show that she wasn't playing.

"No problems, ma." He coughed and spit more blood out of his mouth. "Son pulled his tool out on me. I let him talk his shit, that's where he went wrong, he wanted to talk not act. Peewee had seen Justice running. He called and told me he was going around the back of the building." Bogus sighed; he didn't know if the next statement would end his career or not.

"I told the nigga to do his thing. He hung up on me. I figured he was going to go about his business, and freeze like all the rest of these little niggas. That was until I heard the crack of a pistol. I looked up, the sky was too clear to be lightning. I knew that Peewee might have shot but at no point did I think he would kill him. They were best friends, Simfany, he left little man there leaking over a bitch. I didn't know about the situation with the girl until after Justice was gone. I looked for Peewee to find out what the bloodshed was for. I asked–" Bogus's voice started to go out. He coughed, trying to get the bold clots from the back of his throat. When he finally got it, he spit the blood into the puddle at his feet. He looked up at Simfany.

"I asked him what made him body his man off. He said that I gave him the green light to do it. I gave him the "approval" as he called it to smoke a homie. But he later told me that the real issue was that Justice was fucking with his ex. I made it my business to kill Peewee because it was the only way that I could be linked to the murder of Lil' Jus. I made it look like he killed himself from guilt. Every man for they selves, right? Ain't that how you play the game? Now are you going to let me go or are you going to kill me?" He cut through the bullshit and asked the million dollar question. Simfany smirked.

"A bitch can keep her word." She walked behind the chair that held Bogus tied down, she used the army looking blade to free him from his bounds. Simfany grabbed the rope and walked out the room, leaving Bogus for dead. Simfany hopped in the rental she purchased for the occasion. She was on her way back home to Baltimore County as if nothing had ever happened. Life was great. *Rest in peace, baby boy*, she thought as she pulled away from the curb.

Chapter Seven

Santana stayed awake that night pondering what kind of life he wanted to lead in Charleston. Nobody knew about his past and he wanted to keep it that way. But he continued to ask himself the obvious question over and over again, was he willing to indulge himself back into the game? He played each situation out to the T, all of them leading to jail or death. At the age of sixteen that seemed to be his destiny. Doing a life bid or dead to another nigga's pistol. *Nah, fuck that. I'd do life before I let a nigga smoke me*, he promised himself. Santana sat up. The couch he was laying on felt like a jail mat. He wasn't tired anyway; he was actually wide awake. How he saw it, he would just play his cards as they were dealt.

"Hey, sexy," his thoughts were interrupted by Raven peeking around the wall into the living room.

"Damn, ma, what you tip toeing around in this muthafucka for or am I that off point?" he asked playfully, but seriously questioning himself.

"Maybe both. What's up though? Long time no see. I didn't get to catch up with you much since you been here. But you know how mommy time gets. All day job with no breaks. How you like this little city in West Virginia?" Raven asked.

"The Westside is okay. I'm more of an Eastside nigga if I say so myself!" he said proudly. The look she gave him was confusion.

"Nigga, this is the East end of the city." Now he was the one with the look of confusion on his face.

"I thought this was West Virginia."

"Oh, you a stupid nigga." She laughed. Santana turned beet red; he was embarrassed.

"I apologize, Santana, but nah, West Virginia is its own state, and I thought I was drunk."

"You are or you wouldn't be talking to me like this. It's cool though. You can have ya fun, you big head ass nigga."

"Take it back." Raven laughed some more.

"Nah, because you rude as hell." Raven sat down next to Santana.

"My bad. I was just playing, baby," she stated as she wrapped her arms around his shoulders.

"Shit, you good, ma, I know now. I been calling this the Westside for the last week now. Ya brother a lame for not telling me. Wait till I see that nigga." Raven ran her fingers along Santana's earlobe.

"My G, what you think you doing?" Santana moved over to the far end of the couch. The look she gave him was of pure lust.

"I'm welcoming you West by God Virginia." She attempted to move closer to Santana, but each time he made sure he put more and more distance in between them until he was completely standing. He couldn't run no more.

"Please chill, it ain't that kind of party, Raven. Go to bed. You drunk." He walked over to where she sat and out reached his hand to help her to her feet. She gladly took his hand and rubbed the top of his hand. Raven wanted to flick Santana; that was obvious to the both of them, but Santana wanted to just get his mind right, he had a lot on his plate.

"Raven, please stop." He pulled his hand away from her.

"What? I don't look good enough? Santana, I see how you look at me. Come get some of this pussy." Raven continued to come at him. Santana realized it was a lost attempt to get Raven to stop, so he did the only thing that was plausible. He walked off leaving Raven's drunk ass on the couch in the living room. It was late, but to him it was still early. He walked into the kitchen and waited a second to make sure Raven hadn't followed him. He pulled his Glock off his waist and checked the clip. He was still fully loaded. He knew no one had access to his gun, but he checked it anyway out of pure habit. Santana didn't want to sit in the house no more; he needed to get out. His thought was to just walk around the East, sight-see kind of. He might even slide through Chamberlain Court to see what's up with the old head he met earlier that day. Plus he wanted to see what the after hour money looked like. He walked to the coat rack near the door and put his hoody on. He hated coats; they were too heavy.

Santana liked to be mobile at all times. He peered into the living room and Raven was gone. She was probably either upset or embarrassed, shit, or probably both. Fuck it, it is what it is. After he made sure everything was everything, he turned the lock to leave out the door, but it was already unlocked. That meant that the door had been opened the whole time. Man, Raven tripping, she got niggas sitting duck, duck, goose in this bitch. He made a mental note to check her about that. He opened the door. The February air felt good. It wasn't too cold, but also not warm enough. Santana stepped out of the house and closed the door. He made sure that the slam lock was on, locking himself out. He knew to knock if he had to. He pulled his hood over his head and began to walk down Jackson Street in the direction of the Roosevelt Center.

The Roosevelt Center sat on the corner of Jackson Street and Ruffner Avenue. Police cars aligned the side streets of the Center. He would later find out that the Charleston Police Department had a subdivision attached to the Roosevelt Center. Chamberlain Court sat right behind the Roosevelt in an alley. The dimmed lights didn't help with the sight at night. He figured people knocked the lights out because of the small holes that shown through. Santana walked down the alley like street just observing and taking mental notes. He realized Charleston was filled with a lot of murderous cuts and alleys. He didn't know if niggas from this city thought like that, but he knew what he would use them for if need be. Chamberlain Court was dark. Santana grabbed his Glock off his hip and put it in the pocket of his hoodie. *Just in case, I might scare somebody.* Santana's thoughts were running wild already. Piru fucked his head up with that murder shit. Piru taught him too much, and between Bogus and those T.T.P. niggas—they created a monster. What made it the craziest was that Santana loved the feeling of it all. Out of all the things that ran through his mind, he never once blamed Simfany for the man he had become. His mother did no wrong in his eyes.

"That you there, Souljah?" A voice called from one of the porches. Santana began to walk gain, the voice had some familiarity to it but he couldn't place it, it was enough to keep his gun in his pocket.

"Souljah, where you going?" Santana stopped at the recognition of the old drunk's voice, but this time he sounded much younger.

"Where you at, old head?" Santana looked around until he saw the cherry of a cigarette glow in the night. Santana jogged over the porch and looked up to make sure it was who he thought it was. The man

Jamel Mitchell

looking back at him, he'd never seen before.

"My bad, my G, I thought you was somebody else." Santana was about to leave, but the man stopped him in his tracks. He laughed.

"Nah, souljah, it's me. The old drunk you was going to pay to sight-see with you." The man laughed again. That made Santana mad.

"Fuck you laughing for, my nigga? I can't understand what's so funny!" Santana exclaimed as he tightened his grip on the handle of his Glock 27.

"I just find it funny, souljah, that's all. Don't be mad at me because you let me fool you. Truth be told, you need to pat yourself on the back, you saved a soul earlier. You gone quit crying or you going to come fuck with a nigga?" the man said flatly. Santana went against his better judgment and ascended the stairs onto the porch.

"What's poppin', my G? I'm going to be all the way real with you, this shit awkward as fuck, because ya voice match the drunk's, and my nigga, you a whole different person. What type of shit you on?" The man laughed again.

"Kill-or-be-killed kind of shit. Earlier was you listening to the shit I was telling you? This shit ain't no game out here, but you already know that. I told you, souljah, I saw it in your eyes. I know what taking a soul feels like and by the look of them eyes you do too. Ain't no need to tell me if I'm right or wrong. Real nigga to real nigga though, souljah, I know. Sit down, enjoy the breeze, it's going to be cold for the rest of the week." The man took another pull from his cigarette and inhaled deeply. Santana took in what the man said, but being so off point was what was fucking with his mental. He didn't know if it was because he just wanted to be a kid again or if he really just sleeping on these niggas out here. He promised himself whatever it was, it wasn't going to happen ever again.

"Souljah!" The man snapped his fingers.

"Souljah!" The man waived his hand in front of Santana's face.

"Yo," Santana snapped out of his temporary daze.

"Damn, Souljah, what had your mind gone like that? I been over here trying to get your attention for five minutes. Come inside, the police is riding around." The man opened the door and walked in his home, leaving Santana on the porch. Santana cradled his head in his hands and took a deep breath. He had to get his mind right; it was a must. Santana got up and followed behind his new associate. The inside of the home was nice. The layout was smoove, Santana had to admit. Big screen TVs, and nice furniture, the old head was living good.

"What's up, Souljah? You thirsty? Juice, water, soda—I got it all. If you want you can have that 40.02 you bought a nigga earlier. I don't drink. That was apple juice in the other 40.02 you saw in my hand. Gotta be on point, you feel me, Souljah?" Santana understood clearly. He almost got caught in the middle of some bullshit. Santana sat down. He had a lot of questions to ask.

"So you gone tell me what's up with the whole drunk nigga look or do I have to guess?" Santana said snidely. The man laughed and let the comment roll off his back.

"I told you, you saved a soul today," the man answered as he too sat down on the couch. The man turned the TV on; it was already on Sports Center broadcasting the top ten plays of the night before. The man muted the TV so he and Santana could build.

"I'm saying you told me that much, at least put me on point about the niggas you beefing with. I can't be around a muthafucka and not know what's poppin', you feel me?" Santana sat back.

"I do, Souljah, I do. I told you I had just got out from a bid for a body. The chump I killed, his family running around talking all that hot shit. When I first got out, they got my cell number, they started calling talking about what they going to do to a nigga. I don't do the phone sex, I'm about action, Souljah. I don't take threats on my life easily. I know that dude's family is from around this side of town, so I'm out there begging for change hoping to catch one of them niggaz lacking. Where I'm from, Souljah, it's get right or get left. A lot of these niggas are hoes but some are bom bred killers. It's hard to distinguish who's who so you take them all with precaution. And my precaution is kill or be killed. You know only one side of the gun, that's why you slip at times. You don't know how it feels to be burned, and until you do you won't understand the true meaning to that weapon you carry. So again God has blessed you with a good deed because you saved somebody's life." All Santana could do was nod as he listened. He was all ears, it seemed like no matter where he went he couldn't escape the lite.

"So what you planning on doing tomorrow?" Santana asked.

"Beg for change," Santana laughed.

"I know that's right. What you call yourself, old head?" Santana said sarcastically.

"My niggas call me N.O., you know, short for New Orleans," the man replied.

"You already know my name. How long you do on that body?" Santana wanted to get a demographical look on what the time in prison for playing with that pistol can get you.

"Ten years. I got charged with two-degree murder. They gave me twenty with a mandatory discharge. Down here you do half of your time for the discharge. Bodies down here cheap in the system, now that robbery shit they band a nigga for, so watch out for them kind of charges. The body I caught was on some bullshit. You hear me, Souljah. One night me and my team go to the club, I stumble outside to piss and one of these Charleston niggas got the chop stick in my man's face. I sober up fast and grab the stick. I came back and burned two niggas; one die, the other live to tell all. At first, nobody knew who it was that burned them two niggas, but later found out by one of my souljahs running they mouth to a bitch. Long story short, I get jammed, my brethren go back home and leave me stuck. All but one, my Souljah Frato. He looked out until he got killed back home. So what's ya story?" N.O. asked Santana.

"Ain't no story, my G. Just don't know how to behave. Don't get it fucked up though, my gun bust too. So what's up? You want me out there with you tomorrow or what? My Glock can come in handy if needed." Santana was serious. He missed the rush of feeling that blast from the gun each time he pulled the trigger. He was definitely willing and ready to kill again. Good cause or not.

"Souljah, just heed the warnings. I told you the blue print to the niggas out here. They play for keeps just like every other city in the world." N.O. changed the channel to ESPN Classics. The Bulls was playing somebody; he couldn't make out the other team. His focus wasn't on basketball or TV.

"You know who the dude Zachariah is?"
"You talking bout that little souljah around your age? Pretty boy, long hair looking nigga?" He laughed at his own joke. Then he looked at Santana and laughed even harder. Santana started laughing too with his silly ass.
"Fuck you laughing at?" Santana managed to get out. "You stupid." He laughed some more.
"You—You pretty boy, long hair looking nigga too!" N.O. busted out laughing again. "Truthfully you two lil' souljahs look like brothers."
"I ain't met homie yet; my cousin talk about that's his right-hand man and shit. Just kind of wanted to know what kind of nigga he is." Santana stated.
"Zach, Souljah, about that money. He not a gun play type of nigga. The youngin alright in my book. Don't get it flicked up; the young souljah will protect himself and the people he love. As a matter of fact he probably standing on Lewis Street right now getting that late night money.
"Trying to swing through there?" Santana shrugged.
"Why not, ain't nothing else to do. I'm locked out my spot anyway."
"You gotta leave your stick here though. The police might—" N.O. tried to finish. Santana interrupted.
"Nah, I don't go nowhere without my strap. Fuck these police. I rather be caught with it than without, I know you can understand," Santana explained.
"I feel you, Souljah, I feel you. I was just putting you on point."
"Good looking, but I'm good. Never know when this muthafucka might come in handy." He tapped his hip.
"I don't go nowhere without mine, I just threw that out there to see what you would say. I already know it's shit you're not telling me, but it's all love, Souljah. The eyes tell ya story. Listen, though I told you about the niggas I' m beefing with, it's on sight with me and I'm pretty sure it is with them also, so be on point when you with me." N.O. turned the TV off and got up off the couch. He grabbed the keys that were on the stand closest to the door. Santana was right behind

him as they made their way out the door into the night. N.O. put his hand on Santana's chest for a second. He looked down both sides of the alley to make sure nobody was coming or going. Plus if any bullets was fired he didn't want Santana to fall victim to his beef.

"We good. Walk or drive?" N.O. asked Santana.

"I'm rocking with you, old head." The name was stuck in his head. In all reality the nigga had him by at least ten years, or so he thought. He laughed at the old head shit Santana kept shooting his way.

"Drive, Souljah." N.O. walked up Jackson Street to a newer model Buick LaSabre. It had all black rims with specks of gold in them. The Buick was mean; it screamed money. They walked up to the car and got in. The inside of the Buick was the meanest though. The interior was all black with gold trim. The New Orleans Saints logo was embedded in the head rest of each seat. A medium size TV rested in the middle of the roof, (where the car light usually sat) Santana liked what he saw. N.O. turned the car on and pulled off. The Buick rode so smoothly. He made a mental note to buy a Buick when he got his bread right. Santana tilted his seat back and enjoyed the ride. Lewis Street was located at the other end of the court; it was the street that connected directly to the bottom of Chamberlain Court, while Jackson Street connected to the top. Santana watched as the street lights went by. The car came to a slow stop. N.O. rolled his window down.

"Where the lil' souljah Zach at?" he asked one of the friends walking past. The drug addict stopped.

"What I get out this?"

"I'm just trying to find my lil' homie. Nothing more, nothing less." The fiend walked off; he wasn't willing to get involved in anything unless he was paid for it, no matter the circumstances. N.O. stopped another smoker after he couldn't get the first one to help.

"You know where lil' Zach at?"

"He over Keke's crib with Rodney," the fiend answered and kept moving. N.O. looked over to Santana.

"That's why it's a must you stay on point out this bitch because lives can have a price. They'll tell you anything without knowing they telling anything of value. If we was looking for him and the nigga Rodney, they would be a memory tonight," N.O. explained, trying to show Santana how dangerous a small slip can get you.

The apartment buildings that were neatly tucked away on Lewis Street did numbers, day and night. Santana and N.O. walked past two houses and past at least four to five dope fiends looking to get a fix. Everything from crack, pills, and pussy was being sold or generated around these apartments. Locals playfully self-proclaimed it to be a rendition of "The Carter"—from the hood classic, *New Jack City*. The one thing that Santana took note about more than ever was the lighting. There was none. As he walked deeper into the apartment's court, he clutched his Glock tightly, just in case. He couldn't forget that he was out of town and out of place. This was not his city. He knew being on point, loaded and strapped was his only way of survival. Especially around niggas he didn't know. N.O. stopped at the fourth house. Santana stopped and laughed. He looked down the row of homes and only saw four. The door read: *Apartment Five*.

This shit looked stupid as hell to him. He shrugged it off. At this point, he just wanted to get out of the dark. He was beginning to become paranoid. N.O. knocked on the door.

"Who is it?" a female voice asked from the other side of the door.

"N.O." The door locks clicked and opened, revealing a short skinny woman. She wasn't much too look at but she was fresh. Santana had to give her that. Once Santana got inside, the comfort of the house eased him.

"Keke, what's good, momma?" N.O. said as he hugged her and walked into the living room.

"I'm good. And who is this? Nigga, do I know you? What are you doing in my house? Hello, have I seen you before? Nigga, can you hear me?" she exclaimed and sighed. Santana laughed at her. Keke was on his ass, which she had all right to be; it was her shit. Santana could see through the bullshit though. She was feeling him, which was obvious. He looked at her standing there in the doorway of the living room with her hands on her hips. She was a hood rat for sure.

"Nah, this my first time in ya city, ma," he said to her. Keke rolled

55

her eyes and walked off, putting more sway into her skinny little hips than she had to.

"Where Zach at?" N.O. asked.

"In the living room watching TV with Rodney."

"Good looking. Come on, Souljah." N.O. led the way into the living room. Santana put his hand in his pockets. The touch of metal made him comfortable again. At this point in his life his Glock.27 was the only nigga he wholeheartedly trusted.

"What's up, Souljah? Out here again on a late night. Gotta give it to you, nigga, you 'bout that skrilla. What you make so far?" N.O. asked as he dapped Zach up.

"A couple hundred. It's slow tonight. I was about to bounce for real. What's up? Who the homie you got with you?" Zach asked, looking up from the TV.

"This my lil' souljah Santana. He ya people's cousin. What's his name, the nigga with the sexy ass momma? Kat, I think her name is."

"Oh, that's Montez Cousin. What's poppin, bruh?" Zach replied.

"That's five, what's poppin?" Santana replied.

"Oh shit, we got another slob ass O.T. nigga down here!" Santana turned around so fast to see where the comment came from.

"Rodney, chill out with that slob shit nigga. I told you 'bout that shit, bruh!" Zach stated firmly.

"Fuck them out of town niggas!" Rodney spit venomously. Santana laughed at the kid. He could see it now, him and that Rodney nigga wouldn't like each other.

"I know that's right." Santana laughed. He couldn't wait for a nigga to give him a reason to bury them. Rodney was itching for attention; attention he damn sure didn't want. Santana locked Rodney in his mental. It was no way he could forget this ugly ass nigga with glasses. *Let that nigga get out of line and I'm going to make an example out that ass.* N.O. looked over and shook his head.

"Y'all niggas chill out." N.O. tried. For Santana it was too late.

"That nigga got it, my G, I don't want no smoke," Santana replied as he looked Rodney in his eyes as he spoke each word. "All that arguing is for the birds." Santana and Rodney mugged each other. Neither man wanted to take their eyes off the other.

"Come on, Souljah, we out." N.O. grabbed Santana around the shoulder and spun him around. Santana looked at Rodney one last time and nodded. He bit the bottom of his lip till he tasted blood. He knew what he was going to do to that nigga.

"Calm down, Souljah, fuck that lil' nigga. He ain't 'bout that action. He just getting his voice back. A nigga just ran down on him and popped his stomach all up. Fuck that nigga. He a shooting target out this bitch. He know what time it is!" N.O. said, trying to calm Santana down. Santana walked with N.O. out the door, but his thoughts were on how he wanted to bury Rodney's bitch ass. When Santana looked up, Zach was sitting on the hood of the Buick waiting for him and N.O.

"Nigga, if you don"t get the fuck off . . ." Zach jumped off the hood of the Buick. The snapping sound it made, made N.O. crunch.

"My bad, bruh, it ain't hurt nothing. That shit clean though." Zach laughed. Santana liked Zach; he seemed like he was a cool nigga. He wasn't like the rest of the young niggas he grew around. Zach had a sense to him. He was just one of them niggas, good-hearted. But his man, Rodney—oh, Santana had a clip for that nigga.

"You want me to fuck you up, I can see it now. Nigga, stay off my car." Santana was laughing at the pair, when he looked down the block and saw a car on a slow creep. Before he had a chance to warn Zach or N.O. the passenger side window was opened and a dark figure popped out slightly hanging out the window, strap raised. He knew what time it was; they was on old head's top. He pulled his Glock out as the bullets started to ring. Santana raised his gun and banged back at the speeding car. N.O. turned around instinctively after the first shot was fired.

"This what I been waiting on!" Santana heard N.O. say. N.O. grabbed his gun and started shooting from behind his Buick. Santana squeezed his clip until the immediate threat was through. Santana looked for Zach, but that nigga was nowhere in sight. He looked down in a split moment and saw the bottom of a shoe, most likely Zach's. *Youngin' gone have to wait*, he thought as bullets hit everything around him. Santana took cover behind the Buick. The car sped past, leaving empty shell casings scattered along the street.

"Old head, you good?" Santana called back from behind his hiding spot. Santana needed to check his magazine; he knew he only had three bullets left if he counted right. He pulled out the clip; the shell indicator showed three remaining bullets. "Man, fuck! Fuck! Fuck!"

"I'm good, Souljah, where Zach at?"

"I'm good. What the fuck was that?" Zach asked from halfway under the car. Santana laughed. *This nigga crazy, man.*

"Nigga, get out from under the car, hurry up! We got to go." N.O. yelled at Zach. All three men hopped in the bullet-ridden Buick.

"Fuck—Fuck! Fuck!" N.O. sped off. He knew the cops were on their way. He knew the police quarters were only a block away. So getting somewhere and police-free was all that was on his mind.

"Zach, you good? What about you, Santana, you straight? Good looking back there, youngin'. Them niggas had the drop on me!" he said in a state as if he couldn't believe it himself. Santana looked at Zach and shrugged. N.O. started laughing, but neither Santana or Zach knew why; wasn't nothing funny about the situation.

"Santana, you going home? What about you, Zach?" he asked as he looked in the rear view mirror.

"I told you I'm locked out. I'm mobbing!" Santana replied.

"Drop me off on Lewis Street. Right there near that maroon Camry." Zach pointed. N.O. had circled the block twice, he was tripping. He knew the police would be out soon. Surprisingly there were no police in sight. N.O. pulled up to the front of the house.

"Be safe, N.O., for real, bruh, be safe," Zach said before he opened the door and got out. He shut the door and bent down into the passenger side window.

"Bruh, you can stay the night over here if you locked out," Zach said to Santana.

"I'm good, my G, I'm mobbin' with the homie." Santana almost called him old head.

"A'ight, bro. Be safe then, my nigga." Zach walked off up the way. N.O. looked over at Santana.

"Souljah, rest ya mind here, I'm good. This my war, not yours, but I appreciate the love."

"But I got you, my—" Santana tried to finish, but N.O. didn't let him.

"It ain't about that, Souljah, I can tell you don't listen to too many people. But hear me, go with Zach, he good peoples. Plus I'm about to go set some shit on fire around this muthafucka. Go, Souljah." Santana looked old head in his eyes; he was serious. Santana shrugged and got out the Buick. He turned to close the door, but N.O. sped off down the block. Santana stood in the middle of the street until the car lights disappeared.

"Bruh, come on, if you're coming." Zach tried to yell softly from the door of his home. Santana looked up and without a second thought he jogged up the stairs and into the house.

"Good looking, my G—" Santana said. Zach put a finger over his lips to hush Santana up.

"My bad," Santana mouthed back silently. He followed Zach up the stairs; they stopped at the top of the landing. Zach bent over to wake the dog that lay at the top of the stairs.

"Come on, Moca. Come on, girl." Zach tickled the dog to life. Santana sat there and watched Zach mess with the dog, but he also looked around. It was too dark to make out anything, but a couple of white doors. To the left of the stairs a door was slightly ajar. Right across from the stairs was another room; that door was closed. But a little down the hall was another room, door wide open but no other details were visible. That was all he could make out from where he was standing. Zach patted the dog on the butt to make her go on, so they could get up the stairs. She moved along, letting them up the rest of the remaining stairs. Zach opened the door to the right, and Santana followed; it was another set of stairs leading up into an attic. Santana expected the attic to look old and have a million boxes stored everywhere, but as he walked the final flight, he realized it was another room with a bed and dresser in it.

"This is the guest room, bruh. Make ya self at home. Just don't make too much noise. My parents down there sleeping. What kind of gun you got?" Zach asked.

"A Glock.27," Santana replied proudly.

"Nah, I mean the caliber. I might have some shells somewhere for you."

"It's a .40."

"I'll be back, bruh, give me a couple of minutes." Zach walked back down the stairs and disappeared into the darkness. Santana looked for a switch to cut the lights on, but he couldn't find one. *Fuck it*, he said to himself as he sat on the bed. He sat on the bed and thought about the situation that had just taken place, and he couldn't get that bitch ass nigga Rodney out his mental. If he knew that he could have gotten away with killing Rodney at Keke's house, he would have hit his head. *Chill, that shit ain't 'bout nothing.* He tried to convince himself to calm his nerves, but he knew what he was capable of. He was nobody to these people, and he saw tonight that he would have to put it down to get respect in this city. Instead of preparing to live a normal life, he quickly reverted back to the demon he was. That was Santana's kind of language; he would be prove to be deadly if pushed. Santana looked toward the steps; he heard the wood in the stairs creak. Somebody was on their way up the stairs. Santana grabbed for the gun on his waist until he heard Zach speak.

"Bruh, I'm coming back up, you good?" Zach asked as he peeked his head around the corner.

"Yeah, I'm straight, my G." Zach came up the steps holding a small TV with a cable around his neck.

"Here, bruh, I brought you this TV because you might not be able to sleep tonight. It's already close to 3 a.m. I still got to go to school in the morning. Do ya thang up here. If you get hungry, the kitchen is on the first floor in the back. Just keep the noise down. You good?" Zach asked Santana.

"Yeah, good looking, my nigga. I appreciate it," Santana replied as he grabbed the TV and cord from Zach.

"My bad, homie, I almost forgot." Zach reached into his back pocket and pulled out a box of .40 caliber shells.

"It's only like twenty bullets in this. These going have to do, bruh." Zach reached the box out for Santana to grab.

"My nigga," Santana smiled as he grabbed the box of ammo.

"In the A.M. bro." Zach walked down the stairs.

"The A.M." Santana looked for a light switch again once Zach was gone. He didn't have to look too long because he found a switch close to a closed door. *Damn, how many rooms this muthafucka got?* Santana shook his head. Santana flicked the light on, lighting the attic up. He opened the door in front of him. The room was empty with a window in it that faced the front of the house. Santana looked out the window just out of curiosity. He saw the dark night of Lewis Street. He walked out the room and closed the door. He slid the dresser forward to see if there was a cable box behind it. Luckily for him, there was a cable box there. Santana hooked up the cable into the wall. He slid the dresser back as quietly as possible, then made all the connections to set up the cable. He cut the TV on; the picture was clear. *BET* was playing one of the newest videos of the year. Santana changed the channel to ESPN. He loved sports, so whenever he did look at the television, it would be sports that he watched.

He walked back to the bed and sat down on it. The comfort of the mattress made him tired altogether. Santana looked at the box of bullets that he sat on the bed next to him. He thought about putting more bullets into his gun; he was weird like that. Plus it would leave him something to do for the next day. He put his gun and the box of bullets under his pillow and laid down. ESPN was talking about this year's all-star weekend. Santana closed his eyes as he listened to the sports analyst argue about who was going to win the damn contest this year around. That was all Santana could remember before he fell into a deep slumber. Santana woke up to somebody tapping the bottom of his feet.

"Wake up, bruh. Ya people's been looking for you." Zach sat at the end of the bed.

"Fuck them. Holla at me when you come back from school," Santana said and pulled the cover over his head.

"A'ight." Zach waited a couple of seconds and began tapping Santana's foot again.

"Nigga, go to school," Santana said from under the covers.

"Bruh, I'm back. School's over. Now get your lazy ass up. It's 5:40 in the evening. You slept the whole day." Zach tapped Santana yet again.

"Meet me downstairs in ten minutes." Santana felt the bed adjust to the relief of Zach's weight. Santana stretched while still under the covers. He took a deep breath and exhaled. Now he was awake. *It better be dark outside or I'm gone fuck that little big nigga up.* Santana pulled the cover off of him as he sat bolt upright. Instinctively, he felt under the pillow to make sure his gun was still in place. The box and gun were still under the pillow. Santana didn't have to go far to see it was dark out, the attic window had no curtains so he saw it was night time off on one glance around the room. *Damn I must have been exhausted.* He got up and began getting himself together. He grabbed the box of shells and his gun from under the pillow and sat them side by side of each other. Santana put his sneakers on, put his gun on his waist, grabbed the bullets and made his way down the stairs. He didn't know who was in the house, so he put the bullets in his back pocket.

Zach was chillin' in his room when Santana opened the door to the second floor. Santana remembered the room from last night. It was the only door that was opened all the way. The house was a nice one, Santana had to admit. Zach looked up and motioned for Santana into the room. Santana obliged. He walked into the room and found a seat.

"What's poppin,' bruh? What had you so tired?" Zach looked up at Santana.

"To tell you one thing though, that bed—nigga, that shit the truth. I have to get me one of those soon as I get my own spot."

"What ya money situation looking like right now?" Zach asked. Santana thought hard about the answer he wanted to give.

"What money, my nigga? I'm living in a house with four other mouths to feed, not including mine. My ribs touching, playboy." Santana lied. He knew money made niggas as well as bitches flock to you.

"I fuck with ya peoples, so you my people too. Now I can either give you some money and you can grind with it or blow it. It's on you but understand, nigga, it's all bad over here too. I got two hundred and fifty dollars for you, bro, here." Zach pulled the money out his pocket and counted $250 from it and handed it out for Santana to take.

"Nah, my nigga, I can't take that. I'm good. I know how to survive, son. I definitely appreciate the gesture. That's love." Santana pushed his hand back. Zach looked at him. No words were spoken, but Santana's reaction spoke volumes.

"Take the money, bruh, please, I can't be a nigga that say I fuck with you and you running around this bitch ribs touching. I'm broke too, nigga. These ones in my lap, bruh." He picked the money up in his hand. "This money doesn't mean shit to me. I might have seven hundred dollars to my name, but two hundred and fifty dollars of it is yours. So please take it, bruh." Santana reached out and took the money.

"I'm trying to get some money, son, so who I gotta holla at to get some raw?" Zach burst out laughing.

"What's funny?" Santana was lost.

"Raw what?"

"Heroin."

"Don't nobody sell heroin, bruh, all we got is yay. Crack—But I got a nigga that sell a little weight. His name's Rock. He an a'ight type of nigga, plus the prices are alright. I'ma holla at him tonight for you and let him know we peoples."

"That's cool." The look on Santana's face said he was everything but cool. Zach saw his face instantly.

"What's up, bruh?" Zach asked inquisitively. Santana came straight out with it.

"You gotta show me what I'm doing with this crack shit. I never sold drugs before, my nigga. You see what type of action I'm about. Don't laugh, and teach me what's what so I can get to this money right. My pops had my hood on smash when I was little; it's in my blood to get this money. But we all have to learn the basics, you feel me?"

"I feel you. That's real nigga shit too, bruh. An average nigga would have gone out there and fucked the money up." Zach smiled.

"I told you I ain't no average nigga, blood. You homie too, right?" Santana asked. How Zach had acted the night before over Rodney's comment told him a lot.

"And you know it."

"What hood you bang?"

"I be that Almighty Zoo keeper holding for a helva hot set, BBA foreva teck gang... Eastside till my death."

Santana smiled big. "Okay. Okay. I be that almighty Looney Ru T.T.P 400 block Spruce Street. My 1020 be Piru Flame, his 1020 be that almighty Hood Ru. Bang in peace to the fallen." Santana threw up his hood proudly.

"I can feel you, my nigga, you ready to get to this money?" Zach asked him.

"You already know." Santana and Zach dapped up, bringing their fingers into a perfect five point star. It was their way of showing love to each other and their gangs. But that hand shake also formed a bond between the two men that death couldn't even come in between.

Chapter Eight

Simfany was back in Baltimore and loving every minute of it. She even had Paris with her; surprisingly, but true. Simfany had to admit she liked Paris. What Paris did with that voicemail the day she killed Jimdog really gave her no choice but to give the girl the benefit of a doubt. Paris had all the information any law enforcement would have ever needed. So, Simfany made sure she at least kept in touch with the girl.

"So, girl, what you been doing lately? How my precious Shakira doing?" Simfany asked as they sat in her Tahoe in front of a new club that 92.Q advertised all week. That's how much it meant to her about being out in the night. She couldn't even remember the name of the club. Paris had called and wanted to spend more time with her, so she agreed.

"Nothing with my momma. I'm glad you came and picked me up. I was bored to death." Paris smiled as she looked into the rear view mirror. The gesture was quick; nonetheless, Simfany caught it. Simfany's instincts kicked in. She pulled away from the club; she silently prayed that no one would follow her. Her prayers went unanswered that night because as soon as she pulled away from the curb, so did an all-black Lincoln Town Car. She continued to look in the driver side mirror to see if the Lincoln was still following her as she turned down yet another block. The Lincoln turned the corner with her.

"Simfany, what are you doing?" Paris asked.

"Taking precautions, baby. Taking Precautions." *That bitch the enemy, ma, I swear, I'm sleeping with the enemy.* Simfany could hear Santana's voice almost clearly from the argument they had about Paris. Simfany looked over at Paris; she looked as innocent as a puppy. Simfany couldn't believe what was happening. *Bitch, yeah, you can, you killed her baby daddy,* Simfany thought as she put her foot on the pedal and sped up. She looked at Paris, then looked in the rear view mirror.

"Ma, what are you doing? You're scaring me." Paris buckled her seat belt. Simfany used her right hand to pull her phone out. She pressed and held *2* to speed dial her good friend Carlos.

"Como Estes?" Carlos answered in his thick Spanish accent.

"Los, you got a Lincoln following me tonight?" she asked. She wanted to make sure that she wasn't being followed by one of the twins, Juan and Jesus. They did that often if they spotted her car while in the city. It was the love Carlos had for her that got her those royalties. It was just something about this car following her that didn't feel right.

"No. Why? What's up? Am I needed?"

"Possibly," she replied, looking at Paris out the corner of her eye.

"Where are you now, Chula?" Simfany leaned forward to look out the front windshield; the street sign read *Preston Street*.

"I'm riding down Preston right now," she replied.

"Okay. You know where Bond Street is on Preston?"

"Yeah," she replied instantly. Her pussy was getting wet; she knew that somebody was about to die, and it wasn't her. She had escaped death yet again.

"Go there. Give me two minutes and slide down the block. What does the car following you look like?"

"I'm in my Tahoe."

"No, sweetheart, I meant their car."

"It's a black Lincoln Town car."

"Slow down and breathe. Let up on the gas and breathe. Breathe, Chula, I got you. Are you alone?" Carlos asked.

"No, I got the little girl with me." He sighed heavily.

"You like to play with fire, I see. Listen, when you get to Bond and Preston, drive fast and don't stop until your tail is gone. Call me in ten minutes when they're gone."

"But Carlos—" He hung the phone up. Bond and Preston Street was only a block away. Simfany's hands got sweaty as she turned onto the block. The Lincoln was still behind her. It was now shaking them. Simfany pushed the gas with all her might, shooting her down the block at top speed. Simfany looked in the rear view mirror in hopes of losing her tail, but what she saw took her breath away. Gunfire erupted. The sound of assault rifles woke the hood up for sure.

Simfany slowed down when she saw the quick burst of fire come from the barrels of the men's AK 47's. The Lincoln crashed into a parked car. Nobody inside the car moved. The two men with the assault rifles ran up to the car and emptied the rest of their clips into the town car. Before the two men took off, they looked down the street at the Tahoe. Simfany's eyes were glued to the rear view mirror. When she didn't pull off right away, one of the men waved her on. Simfany snapped out of her momentary shock condition and pulled off. Simfany looked over at Paris. Tears silently ran down Paris face. Simfany couldn't hold the silence anymore.

"Why you crying for?" Simfany laughed.

"Because them people just lost their lives back there," Paris replied hysterically.

"So you would rather lose yours?" Simfany asked seriously.

"How do you know they were going to kill us? You don't!" Paris screamed.

"Hold on, little girl, cut your fucking tone. They followed this car for twenty minutes. What the fuck you so mad about, you little snake ass bitch!" That changed Paris's whole demeanor.

"What you talking about, Simfany." The tears stopped completely.

"My son loved you, but he knew he was sleeping with an enemy of some form. All this over Jimdog? For real. . ." Simfany pulled over.

"Get out!" Simfany yelled at Paris.

"I didn't do anything though," Paris replied.

"I'm giving you your chance to live, you grimy ass bitch. I haven't been inside the city since I killed that bitch ass nigga of yours. That Lincoln been on my ass on and off since Edgewood. So get the fuck out of my car now! I know you called them when I just popped up. You grimy for that, but hey, it's all fair in love and war. Get the fuck out of my car! This is my last time asking you, Paris." Simfany yelled. Paris was so gone off being caught up in her actions that she didn't even realize where she was.

"Get out or die. You choose." Paris hurried up and grabbed her purse when Simfany got to talking about murder. Paris knew that Simfany wasn't playing with her threat. Paris was so nervous that she dropped the contents of her purse on the floor of the car. Paris opened the door to illuminate the light of the car. Before Paris had the chance to put the small gun back into her bag, Simfany saw it. Paris hurried and put the rest of her things back into her purse. She closed the door. Simfany watched as Paris made her way around to the driver side window. What Simfany didn't see was the gun Paris held in her hand. Paris was emotionally distraught.

"Bitch, you just killed both of my cousins. You gone pay for everybody that you have dropped this last—" Simfany held eye contact with Paris while she reached into the center console and grabbed her Glock. Simfany felt around until her hand was able to wrap around the handle of her gun. *Simfany, think, how do you get out of this one?* She cursed herself. The words that Paris was saying meant nothing at the moment; all she thought at the moment was to survive. Simfany rested the Glock on her lap, hoping Paris would take her eyes off her for a split second. All she heard from Paris before Paris raised her gun to eye level was:

"Bitch, you gone die tonight." Simfany saw no other way to survive. She squeezed the trigger until the gun wouldn't bust no more. The sound of the gun being shot from inside the car deafened her. Each shell that went through the driver side door hit Paris in her chest and stomach. The feathers from her *North Face* proved that; each shot that entered her body caused a ruffle of blown feathers in the brisk air. Simfany put her hand on the gear. She was about to pull off until she heard what sounded like a gargling noise. She looked out the window at Paris. Paris wasn't dead yet; she was fighting. The sight was damaging to Simfany; she didn't want to kill Paris. Once Paris threatened her life, she had no other choice but to react in a manner that would keep herself alive. Now Paris lay sprawled out choking on her blood. Simfany started to cry. She didn't know what to do. She knew that she couldn't let Paris live; the consequences that she would have to face were too great. Jail or death wasn't in her cards. She pulled her phone out and called the only nigga she could trust, her son. He answered on the first ring.

"What's up, pretty lady?" Santana answered.

"Quick, let me know what should be done. I'll explain later. Paris is on the ground coughing up her own blood. She pulled on me first." Santana answered immediately without second thought.

"Do your thing. Call me when you calm down." Santana could hear that his mother was all worked up and distraught.

"Love you, baby. And I'm sorry."

"Love you too, ma, go handle ya business. Don't let shorty suffer, for Shakira." Santana hung the phone up. Simfany knew it would hurt Santana to know that she killed Paris. She had no time to think about that though. She reached into her purse and grabbed another magazine for her pistol. She replaced the new clip for the old one. Simfany cocked the barrel, placing a bullet into the head of the gun. She looked around before she opened the door. She looked down at Paris and stepped out of her truck.

"Plea. . .ssss. . .e—he-l-ppp," Paris tried to say as she watched Simfany hop out the truck. Paris gargled some more. Simfany watched as Paris pushed blood out the side of her mouth so she wouldn't drown. Tears unwelcomingly rolled down Simfany's face. She couldn't let Paris live; she shouldn't have back then and she won't now. Paris made this bed of hers, now it's time to lay in it. Game over.

Simfany wiped her face with her sleeve, she upped her Glock and squeezed the trigger. The bullet hit Paris in the left eye, slamming her head into the pavement. She squeezed again, putting a hole in the girl's forehead. Simfany wanted to make sure that it was over with these people. The blood that poured out of the little girl's body told her enough. Simfany jumped back into her Tahoe and sped off. Her body count was rising ridiculously, and she was okay with that; if that meant her and her son could duck the coffin for a little while longer. Her phone rang. She picked it up and looked at the screen; it was Carlos. She answered quickly.

"Hold on, let me jump on this highway real quick," Simfany said as soon as she answered her phone. The caller said nothing, he just waited.

"Okay, I'm sorry, hello?"

"I'm here, so are you okay now?"

"Yes, thank you, Carlos. If it wasn't for you I would have seen a coffin years ago. Thank you for real."

"I told you I got you, Chula. Now what will you do about the little girl?" Los asked.

"Already handled. The little bitch had the nerve to up strap on me. Crazy, huh? You already know it hurt my heart, but it is what it is. But again thank you. I'll call you once I'm somewhere safe. Okay?"

"Okay, Chula, don't be a stranger. If you need me, I'm a phone call away." Carlos ended the call. Simfany turned her music up as she rode home to her one-bedroom Baltimore County town house. Life wasn't all that great, but it could be way worse than what she knew of life. Even though the man upstairs probably didn't fuck with her too tough, she silently said a prayer for Paris's soul. It was the first time she had really prayed since she killed Emilio.

***

"The body of Bernard Tru, better known as Bogus, a highly ranked member of the *Sex, Money, Murder* blood gang, was found slain and mutilated outside of a Queens structural home. We don 't have much information to share, but if you have any information I urge that you call the NYPD. Call 718-555-5961. Reporting live—New York 5 News."

Lonnie watched with satisfaction as the heroin hit her veins, taking her to another familiar place of euphoria.

***

Santana sat in the back of N.O.'s Buick and silently cried for Paris. He loved her, but in the light of the situation it was a must that she be killed. The tears that ran down his face were of frustration. Before Zach or N.O. could look back, he wiped his face. Another soul lost, another sad story. Santana shrugged it off. It is what it is. He put his phone away and looked out the back window.

"What's up, Souljah? You good back there?" N.O. asked as he stared at Santana through the rear view.

"Yeah, I'm good, my G. Somebody I knew got smoked tonight. But it's the life we live. I'm *hundred* though, my nigga. What's up with you? What happened with you last night?" Santana changed the subject.

"I went to a motel," N.O. began his explanation. "I had to clear my mind. I was about to shoot everything up, but I quickly calmed myself. Emotion is a bitch. I didn't want to go do some dumb shit because I was mad. So what I do? I went to clear my mind. In due time I will get my target. Until that time comes I'll be patiently waiting."

"Did you go out today?" Santana asked. Only the two of them knew their inside joke.

"You know it, Souljah, and I got my money up." N.O. laughed his ass off.

"That's what's up."

"Man, what the fuck you two muthafuckas keep laughing about?" Zach asked as he looked up from his phone.

"Money, nigga, we talking about money," N.O. stated.

"You know I'm all for that bread," Zach said, matter-of-factly. Santana laughed.

"You two pretty boy ass muthafuckas, I'm going to call y'all the *Pretty Boy Souljahs*." Santana and Zach looked at each other.

"Man, fuck you!" they said simultaneously. All of them burst out laughing. Santana's phone cut them off. Santana looked at the phone light up on his lap. He wasn't sure he wanted to answer it. The news about Paris had fucked his night up. He really wasn't trying to talk. It could only be a select few that could be calling. Regardless of his feelings, he picked up the phone and looked at who the caller was. It was Kat. He answered his phone without hesitation.

"Hello," Santana said.

"Boy, where you been at? I been worried about you!" Kat said.

"I told Montez I was good earlier," he explained, but he knew right there that his hoe ass didn't tell nobody.

"Oh, okay, nah, he didn't tell nobody shit, with his tall slinky ass." That made Santana crack a smile. "And who you hanging out with that you been M.I.A. for two days?"

"One of the homies. I'm good, I promise. My momma raised a helva nigga!" he said pridefully.

"I understand, little boy, remember my rules. As long as we have an understanding, we're straight."

"I understand, auntie," Santana said sarcastically. "Oh, I almost forgot, who is leaving the door open?"

"I thought that was you that been locking the door. We don't lock the door unless everyone is gone. Even at night I keep it open, I don't know—it's just what we do down here."

Before he could curve his tongue he just spoke.

"Well, that's stupid. I mean—My bad, ma. But ain't that dangerous, Kat?"

"Depends if you look at it that way. You're right. Anybody can walk into my home if my door is open, but people don't. Baby, we don't have nothing here that anybody can want, besides pussy. Other than that reason, people come over here, chill, then leave. No worries, we are loved around here, baby boy."

"Understandable. I didn't mean to lock the door. It was just out of habit." Santana shrugged. The explanation she gave was straight bird brain shit. The only reason he couldn't feel some type of way was because it was her home. He knew from that day on if that door wasn't locked he wouldn't stay there.

"Okay, sweetheart, you be good and stay safe."

"You do the same, keep that damn door locked!" She laughed, but agreed before Santana hung up. He smirked as he sat his phone back into his lap. Kat was a nut, but she was cool as a fan. The passenger door opened, Zach got out to stretch.

"Nigga, close the door, it's cold as shit!" Santana yelled from the back seat. It was crazy how much he and Zach really resembled each other. The only difference between the two was their height, Zach was about 5'10 with one of those Italian noses. Over the years Santana had

grown himself. He was now 5'6, still short, but tall all in the same sense. Zach got back in the car and shut the door.

"So, what's up? What we going to do tonight?" Zach asked.

"It's a school night, Souljah. You got something planned for us?" N.O. asked.

"Nah, I just wanted to know, and so what if it is a school night?

Nigga, I'm grown." Santana laughed from the back seat. Zach looked at him through the rear view. He was riding passenger with N.O.

"You ain't got no yay for me? That nigga Rock ain't been answering his phone. You know how that nigga get with his scary ass!" Zach said.

"I got you. What you trying to grab?" Zach looked back at Santana.

"What you trying to buy, bruh?"

"What the prices looking like?" Santana asked as if he knew what he was talking about.

"A hundred and fifty dollars a ball, two hundred and twenty-five dollars a quarter, four hundred and fifty dollars a half, eight hundred dollars for the onion. But I'll charge you six fifty an onion. Speak now or forever hold your peace!" N.O. replied. Santana was confused. If N.O. had the weight for sale, why was Rock even in the equation? He silently had to ask himself that over and over again. He made a mental to talk to Zach about that.

"Santana, tell me something," Zach said.

"How much you got, son?" Santana asked as he did the quick math in his head.

"I got that four hundred and fifty dollars I had still from earlier. You wanna put that other bread with it and get an onion?"

"N.O., give us three. Nah, as a matter of a fact, make it four. I'm going to need you to drive my cousin spot for a quick minute. I gotta get my money." Zach looked over at him all weird and shit, so Santana turned his seat.

"What, nigga? I told you I kept ya money." Santana smiled as he reached in his pocket and took out the two hundred and fifty dollars Zach had given him only hours earlier. He intended to give the money back a little later because Zach looked out; offering him the money while he was broke meant something to him. N.O. pulled off from the front of Zach's crib and drove around the corner to Kat's house.

"Give me a second. I'll be back." Santana rushed out the car and into the house. Of course, the front door was unlocked. Santana checked the kitchen, dining room, and living room. Nobody was there. He listened for a second, no movement. He walked to the basement door and listened also. Silence. He opened the door and walked down the steps. The basement was empty. No furniture, no boxes, no sign of any life beyond this room. He went to the brick in the wall he had loosened when everyone was gone; this was the spot that he hide his money at. He wiggled the brick out of its place. The roll of money that his mother gave him sat neatly in the back just as he last placed it. He reached in carefully and grabbed the money out; he didn't want any dust from the cement to leave any tell-tale signs of his hidden spot. He took out the $2600 for the "work" and four for himself. That only left him with a little under $1800. If all was to go as planned, he wouldn't have to touch that money at all. He also grabbed ten shells out of his box of bullets. They were hollow tips; he only needed a few to mix in his clip. If his unlucky target got hit by one then so be it; he knew they would get the job done. He placed everything back in place and pushed the brick back into its rightful place. Santana dusted the spot around the brick with his shirt, just in case any dust was left that he couldn't see; he had to take precautions. He walked back up the stairs and out the door. He didn't check to see if anyone was up or not; he just left and locked the door on his way out.

***

Montez heard the door to the basement creak open. He didn't know why, but he hid in the dark to see what was going on. When he saw Santana come from behind the door, it pegged his interest. He looked down at his watch; it was 1:20 in the morning. *Fuck he doing in the basement?* Montez asked himself multiple times. He didn't know but he was about to see. He stood in the dark. He was going to wait for Santana to go upstairs before he went down into the basement, but he heard the front door open and close. Montez now knew that Santana was out the house, so it put him more at ease with what he was doing. Montez ran and locked the door, but Santana had already beaten him to it. It really put Montez at ease to know Santana wouldn't be coming back for the rest of the night. He walked to the basement door and opened it. Montez looked down the dark stairs.

He didn't know what he was looking for. He began to walk down the steps in hopes of finding out why Santana snuck back into the house while everyone was sleeping. Even though it was a fragment of the truth, it was still what motivated his cause. Unbeknownst to Santana of Montez's action, Santana walked to the car and got in.

"Damn, nigga, you said you was going to run in and come back," N.O. complained playfully.

"I had to be quiet—I didn't want to wake anybody," Santana replied.

"Shit, I'm surprised you didn't see Montez. He walked on the porch a minute or two after you got inside. I guess the nigga came out for fresh air, because he was stretching and shit. He might have gone back upstairs. I don't know. If you didn't see him then he might not have seen you either. We ain't park in the front of the house so when he came out he didn't see us either." Zach shrugged, brushing it off. But Santana was hoping Montez wasn't on no bullshit. He would hate to bring harm to Justice's first cousin, but he certainly would. Santana tried to let the thought go by counting out the twenty six hundred he owed for the work. After he finished counting the money, he tapped the driver side headrest. He grabbed N.O.'s attention.

"Here, my G. That's twenty-six. I'll be right back." Santana handed the money to N.O. and got out the Buick, leaving the door ajar. Santana ran to the left side of the house where there was a narrow path paved for neighbors. Santana ran to the small window nearest to the ground and crouched. He looked into the basement and it crushed his heart when he saw Montez looking around in the basement. He didn't need to see nothing else. Santana hopped back on to his feet and ran back to the Buick. He would handle that at a later date.

"We good," Santana said as he shut the door behind him. Without question N.O. pulled off. Zach sat silently in front as he looked out the window. *Fuck wrong with that nigga?* Santana asked himself. When he caught Zach by himself, he made a mental note to see if all was well. N.O. drove them back to Zach's house.

"I'll be back, be on the porch."

"Yup," Zach replied. When Zach opened the door, Santana followed suit. Both boys walked up the steps and sat on the porch as

N.O. pulled away. Santana looked at Zach; he didn't know how to approach the situation. So he just asked what was on his mind.

"My nigga, what's on your mind?" Santana asked Zach.

"That money, you told me you was on ya dick. Bruh, I don't fuck with niggas that lie. You can't trust them kind of people!" Zach replied, but looked away.

"First off, my nigga, I didn't lie to you. That's a bitch emotion that I don't contain. And the only thing we can agree to is your statement that liars can't be trusted. And what the fuck is on ya dick mean?"

"Doing bad, being broke."

"Nigga, I am broke, I just invested two thousand six hundred dollars in "our" come-up, nigga. Fuck you talking about?" Santana thought for a second, it all started to make sense.

"Oh, so you think a nigga got money." He laughed. "Well, nigga you wrong. I live in a house full of people. My raise gave me enough money to survive for two weeks at most. Maybe a little while longer, but I invested more than half in, like I said before, "our" come-up. That two hundred ands fifty dollars you gave me, nigga, made me wanna do that, son. You ain't hesitate with your last, so why the fuck would I? The deal was good, I even knew that and I never sold crack in my life. It's time to get this money, son, so miss me with that emotional shit you spitting out ya mouth. And by the way, your little friend Montez—that nigga might get found in one of y'all rivers around this motherfucker. Especially if that money ain't where it was left."

Zach said nothing. He continued to look off down the street. Pride was a muthafucka, Santana had to admit, as Zach just sat there lost in his thoughts. The awkward silence lasted for a couple of minutes. N.O. pulled up, breaking the silence. *Back to business*, Santana thought to himself. Neither Zach nor Santana had spoken. When Santana saw the black and gold Buick pull up to the curb, he made his way down the steps and approached N.O. Santana jumped in the car. N.O. handed him a bag with crack inside; it was a solid block.

"What you and little homie Zach gone do tonight?" N.O. asked.

"Bag this yay up and get to that money," Santana replied.

"A'ight, I'm out. If you need me, let me know, and I appreciate you. When them niggas had the drop on me, you held me down. Love for that, Souljah."

"No *thank you* needed, my nigga, I got you. That's what a real nigga supposed to do anyway, especially if he not trying to get bodied himself. Good looking on the prices too, son, I'll hit you tomorrow."

"A'ight, Souljah, be safe and stay strapped." The pair dapped each other up. Santana got out the car and walked back onto the porch. N.O. sped off down the block. Santana watched the tail lights of the car till they disappeared.

"I got the work, bro, let's chop this shit up and get this money." Zach got off his ass and opened the door to his home. Santana followed Zach up the stairs silently, until Zach stopped short at the top of the stairs. Moca was at the landing of the steps again. Zach rubbed the dog until it awoke. He patted the dog on the butt until she rose for her spot and walked away. They continued the walk until they were in Zach's room with the door closed.

"Bruh, my bad for—" Santana cut him off.

"My nigga, ain't no need for that. What's understood doesn't need to be explained. Now show me what the fuck I got to do." Santana smiled and pulled the block that N.O. gave him out of his pocket. In the light the block was hefty. Zach grabbed the scale so they could weigh the product. Zach sat the scale on a flat surface and weighed the product. The look on Zach's face told him that something was wrong.

"What's up, my G? Is it short?" Santana asked in disbelief.

"Nah, bruh, it's more. It says 126 grams. That's 4'/1 easy, bruh looked out.

"You got N.O.'s math?" Santana asked.

"Yeah, why? What's up?"

"I'm about to call the homie and let him know that it's more than we paid for."

"Real nigga shit, I ain't even think of it like that. Let me dial it for you, hold on." Zach looked through his phone for the number; when he found it, he dialed it then handed the phone to Santana. Santana grabbed the phone from Zach and set it on speaker.

"Souljah, what's up?" N.O. answered after the first ring.

"Son, my bad for the late call, but my nigga, the bag was heavier than what it was supposed to be," Santana explained. N.O. laughed and replied.

"Yeah, Souljah, I know what was there. I put something extra in there so you and your partner can eat," N.O. explained.

"Oh, a'ight, just needed to know for sure, old head. Good looking out, son. We appreciate it."

"You know it, hit me. Oh, and Zach, I just seen ya little homie a second ago—What's his name—Man, you know who I'm talking about. The little brown skin Souljah was in Tiger Morton for that shooting on the West."

"Who? Haseem?" Zach got excited.

"Yeah, that big eared lil' nigga. I just saw him riding around with Rodney's little ass."

"Good looking. I'm 'bout to be out there in a second. I'll see him."

"Okay, I'm out." N.O. hung up the phone.

"My nigga home! You gone love this nigga!" Zach said excitedly. When he realized he was tripping, he calmed down and got back to the task at hand.

"Let me show you how you get this money." Zach grabbed the blade and plate that was under his bed. He showed Santana what a 20 dollar rock looked like, he also explained that the eye was at most times the best scale. That was unless he was going to bag each rock individually. And Santana being a true New Yorker, he was more into bagging the work up. Luckily, Zach had small baggies to put the 20 dollar stones in. Santana and Zach cut up an oz. in 20's, they both took a half and concealed it somewhere on their bodies. They were ready to get to the money. But if only Santana really understood the hate that would come from the love he and Zach had for each other, he would have chose another city to call home. Santana took the bullets out his back pocket and placed them under some clothes in Zach's top drawer. He made a mental note to put the hollow tip shells in later; at the moment he had full clip and he was good. No worries. He had no worries at all.

***

The rest of the night went exactly as planned, no worries. Santana and Zach both got their assignments off. Santana made $900 while Zach made $1,100. The night was definitely a good one, but Haseem and Rodney were nowhere to be found. Santana was glad he didn't get to run into Rodney because he wasn't too fond of the nigga at all. He knew fuck niggas when he saw them, and Rodney was exactly that. He felt at any moment he was willing to spill shorty's blood. They stayed posted on Lewis Street right across the street from "The Carter" until day break. Sleep wasn't in the cards. Time was of the essence; it was time to get back to the money.

"You going to school today?" Santana asked Zach as they walked down Lewis Street to Zach's house.

"Hell nah, bruh. You see the money that's out right now. I never made $1,100 in one night. That's crazy. For real, bruh, think about it, between the two we made $2 bands in one night!" Zach was excited. They damn near made the money back and still had 3 1/2 oz. waiting on them.

"So what you wanna do? You trying to go back out there?" Santana asked, knowing the answer.

"Yeah, why you not?" Zach looked at Santana crazily.

"Hell yeah. I'm down, son. Put this money away and get to the next level. I also was thinking for ya homie Haseem—we can give son the extra half we got to put him on his feet!" Santana stated as he waited for Zach to unlock the door at his home.

"I'm definitely for that. And bruh—" Zach turned and looked Santana in his eyes. "I didn't mean—nah, I shouldn't have called you a liar. I keep forgetting your circumstances at Montez's. Real niggas can apologize when they are wrong. And true, indeed, bruh, I apologize." Santana laughed.

"Apology accepted, cookie dough, marsh mellow, soft ass high yellow—" Santana was on his top.

"A'ight, nigga, shut up." They burst out laughing. They dapped up, forgetting the situation had ever happened. They walked up the stairs and Moca was laid out on the top of the landing again. Zach had to rub her to wake yet again. To Santana it seemed as if it was a ritual between Zach and Moca; he had to admit the shit was loyalty in a rare form. Santana made a mental note to ask once they settled. After Moca moved to her bedroom, Zach and Santana went in to the room and closed the door. Zach got settled on the bed as Santana pulled out a rolled cigarillo that was filled to its capacity with the best of Charleston's mid-grade weed.

"My G, why every time we walk up the stairs from coming out side, your dog is lying at the top of the stairs?"

"Who? Moca? I had that dog since I was about five years old. She was a puppy then, I was a kid. Bruh, only if you knew, me and Moca used to do everything together. My bitch getting old. When I go out and it turns dark, she looks for me all over the house and when she knows I'm not here, she'll wait up for me until she falls to sleep. I could easily step over her when I come in but I don't want her to worry herself to death. So I make sure I let her know I'm back so she can
sleep peacefully in her own room. That's my baby. If nobody in life loves me, I know she does and will." The clicking of the dog's nails could be heard as she trotted into the room. Santana guessed she had heard her name being spoken about so she made her presence known. When Moca came in, she laid at the bottom of Zach's feet and without hesitation Zach rubbed her.

"Go 'head, Moca, daddy's got company." Moca rose up and barked at him, then left the room. Zach and Moca's bond was impressive.

"Son, did she get a dog attitude with you?" Santana laughed hard. Zach ignored him.

"Now let's get to this money," Zach said. He went to the closet and pulled his fire-proof safe off the shelf that was hidden in the back spaces. He opened it and put his money in the box and grabbed the remaining block of crack out. Santana followed suit and put his earnings in the small safe also. Zach reached under the bed and grabbed the plate and blade that they used to cut the last batch of crack up on. Zach didn't waste no time; he began to break down small pieces that would go for $20 a rock. Santana pulled the baggies out of the safe and started to help his brotha. Once again after the process was over, each man took half of the work out to do what it do. Santana looked at the clock on Zach's dresser, it was 8:30 in the morning and neither man had plans to rest. Santana's adrenaline was rushing from the money that he was seeing in such a quick time. He put his Glock .27 back on his hip and went out the door with Zach in tow; it was time to get back to the money.

***

As Santana walked down Lewis Street, he consciously touched his waist, making sure his Glock was in place. He wore that gun so much that now it felt like an extra piece of clothing. He refused to go any-where without it. Once he felt the bulge at his waist, his mind was set at ease; he knew he was safe by his hand. Zach's phone rang as they walked up the street. Santana laughed because Zach had a weird ass ring tone; he had heard it before but could not picture it at that mo-ment. Zach looked up and his face turned red from embarrassment. He snatched his phone out of his pocket and looked at the incoming call. It was Rodney.

"Man, I know this dumb ass nigga put this lame ass ring tone on my phone!" Zach stated angrily, trying to save face.

"Call my phone real quick, bruh—I wanna see something," Zach said to Santana. Santana pulled his phone out and dialed Zach's num-ber from memory. Zach's phone rang, but a Julez Santana song—"Bandana"—played through.

"That's what I thought," Zach stated as he put his phone back into his pocket. The awful ring tone played again. Zach made no effort to answer his phone; he was tired of Rodney's bullshit. *Fuck Rodney*, Zach thought to himself. As the pair got to the corner of Lewis and Ruffner, the blaring police sirens came out of nowhere. Both of them turned toward the noise; it sounded as if the police were right behind them. When they turned, an all-white Crown Victoria came speeding around the comer. The police was right on the tail of the car.

The Crown Vic stopped suddenly in the middle of the street on Ruffner Avenue, forcing the police car to swerve out the way to avoid a collision. The driver side door opened almost instantaneously, followed by the passenger; two men jumped out the car. Santana recognized one of the men; it was Rodney's sucker ass and some light-skinned dude. Zach took off down the street. Santana wasn't in no hurry especially not with an half of oz. crack in his pocket and a fully loaded gun. That was a dead issue. Against better judgment, he walked up the block to make sure that Zach was good. Rodney hit the cut on the 1500 block of Lewis Street going in to the alley; it was the same alley that was located directly across from "The Carter". If he took the cut all the way out, he would end up on the next street over, 1400 block of Jackson Street east.

When Rodney disappeared, he followed Zach with his eyes wondering what the fuck Zach was doing. He was definitely not about to get close to any scene that involved police and K-9 units. The K-9 decided to chase the light-skinned nigga. The light-skinned nigga tried to hop the fence to get away from the dog, but every fence he hopped—the dog hopped with the same ambition. What Santana couldn't understand was why the man ran into "The Carter"; the court was a dead end. He thought so at least.

Santana would later find out that there is a cut alongside the fence located at the last housing unit. Only moments later, a black police officer was walking a cussing Rodney back through the four-way alley in handcuffs. Santana couldn't hear what was said but Rodney and
Zach exchanged heated words before Rodney was put into the back of the waiting cop car. Santana sat down on the structure brick wall that was on the end of Lewis and Ruffner. He watched as the neighborhood came alive at 8:30 in the morning. The police activity would be talked about amongst people for the rest of the day, if not the rest of the week, depending on what rumors would surface. Every hood had nosey neighbors.

Zach looked over at Santana and shook his head in disbelief; he was pissed and disappointed at the same time. As the police led the second small man out of the small housing development in hand cuffs, Zach followed side by side with them, talking to the police officer. The officer ignored him as he put the other man into the cop car with Rodney. Zach walked off after that; he was defeated. Santana could tell that he was in his bag about something, but he wouldn't comment on it unless it was brought to the floor. Zach said nothing as he looked both ways up and down Ruffner before he crossed the street to where Santana was at. Santana didn't greet him; he just sat there knowing Zach would explain his frustrations. But if he was wrong, so be it; it was none of his business no way. Zach sighed and rubbed his fingers through his hair in frustration. Zach looked up at Santana and shook his head. That gave Santana the green light to show support.

"What's good, my G?"

"Rodney pulled my brother into some bullshit. That nigga, man—oooooh, bruh, I swear," Zach said frustratingly. *This nigga got a brother? Where fuck that nigga be posted at?* Santana just kept his thoughts to himself because at the end of the day Zach having a brother was irrelevant.

"Then this bitch ass nigga gone say that I chose you over him and I was a bitch nigga for real. Bruh, I grew up climbing in trees with that nigga that used to be my best friend!" Zach said, putting an emphasis on 'used to'. "But ever since this nigga got shot that day and survived, he has been on some gangster, Bone Thug and Harmony type shit." Zach had to laugh. "I don't know how to explain it, bruh. Fuck that nigga. That nigga don't want it for real!" Zach vented.

"So what them niggas do anyway?" Santana asked curiously.

"Nothing, really, Rodney had a penchant for some dumb shit, but now them lame ass niggas got felony, fleeing and possession. They're stupid, bruh. Fuck talking bout them niggas. What's up with this money that needs to be made?" Santana smiled. Nothing could stand in the way of Zach and his money, even though those words were just a joke within itself. Zach would later prove that nothing, not even money could override the love and loyalty he had for Santana. Santana dropped the whole police situation with Rodney; it was back to his mission: Getting money.

"Let's get this money then," Zach said as if he read Santana's mind. Zach stood and looked down the street; the crowd started to disperse.

"Say no more. Where you trying to post at?" Santana stood and asked Zach.

"Nigga, it don't even matter. Let's just get to this money, bruh. I need to get this other shit off my head." Santana understood and just went with the flow.

The boys sat on the stairs and caught every sale coming through the cut before they could make it to Keke's trap. That was a trick that Zach had put him onto early into the game. The yay that was combined between the two was gone by the time the school buses came rolling through at 3:30 p.m. *This shit too easy, blood*, Santana thought to himself as he counted his daily earnings. The money that Charleston had to offer was amazing. It was unbelievable the kind of money that Santana made in just one day. On Courtland it was always mayhem, niggas had to have permission period to get any type of ones. Dracula would have his head if he knew what he was doing on another nigga's block. He never got the chance to witness the legend at work, but the stories he heard about his father were of no-nonsense. The day had started off so-so because of the police chase and arrest of his homie's people, but all in all the day had blossomed into a fruitful
one.

The money that was being made should have been the last thing on Santana's mind. Being in a new city brought upon new enemies, and new enemies caused more problems. The streets never slept, and whether he realized it or not, regardless of the jurisdiction, people played for keeps. The only difference now is the prey.

Chapter Nine

Santana and Zach should have won *Hustler of the Year* for the money they made between the two of them in such a short period of time. The money that he began to see was a new feeling of lust. He was locked up since he was thirteen and he missed out on a lot. He fell in love with the feel of holding that pistol in his hand. That became second to Santana's heart besides, first being to Simfany. The feeling of having to eat day today was a feeling he wished and hoped he wouldn't ever feel again. That was a dead issue to him, now and forever. He made a pact within himself during the weeks of him trapping, he would rather be in the penitentiary than be a bum on the corner of a niggas block.

But as work moved and money was collected and spent, Santana finally has a chance to gather his thoughts. This was his time of solace. As he spent time with himself, the disloyalty that he felt was displayed by his cousin resurfaced. That was a sour taste in his mouth all together. He honestly hoped that Montez wouldn't play foul like that. Montez's life depended on it. Santana made a mental note to check on the situation ASAP.

***

Santana opened the door to the basement and walked down the stairs. The emotion that he gathered as he took every step overwhelmed him because he knew he saw Montez in his stash. He prayed that his cousin just looked in the stash, but took nothing. He knew he was asking for ice water in hell too. He continued his walk until he got under the steps where the loose brick was located. Santana looked at the concrete wall to find the lose brick and shook his head at the sight of it. When he first found the spot to hide his money, it was hard to see where one could hide anything, but now as he looked at the wall, it was obvious something was or used to be hidden behind that exact brick. Santana's heart dropped; he knew what time it was. He lifted the brick from its spot and looked into the hole. He knew what he would see so he wasn't surprised when he saw nothing there. Santana let the brick fall from his hand as he walked away leaving his heart and the brick in the same place the floor. Santana's blood boiled as he made his way up the stairs looking for his "cousin". *That bitch nigga ain't nothing like me or mine. I'm sorry, Justice. Please don't hate me for this*, Santana thought as he looked room to room for Montez. He refused to make a scene about the shit, but it was definitely going to be handled. Whether it was now or later it, was going to be handled how he saw fit. Santana had nothing to do but hunt, so he stayed put and waited on Montez to make his way home.

Two hours later, Montez walked through the door with two Young's Department store bags in his hands, carrying the latest Jordan's and another bag full of clothes. It fucked Santana up how careless Montez carried his actions, but he had to realize that Montez didn't know that he was actually caught red-handed stealing from him. Santana took it as a sign that he didn't give two fucks.

"What's good, bruh? Ain't seen you in a while," Montez said as he sat his bags down in the middle of the floor. Santana didn't respond; he just sat and looked at Montez like he was stupid.

"Fuck wrong with you, bruh?" Montez asked like he didn't have a care in the world. The feeling of betrayal and thievery made Santana move quickly and efficiently. Santana rose off the couch and struck Montez in the head with the butt of his gun. Montez fell and his head instantly opened up.

"Get ya bitch ass up, nigga!" Santana ranted as he hit Montez over his head again with his Glock. 27. Santana continued to hit him until he fell unconscious. Each hit threatened to break a bone on Montez's face. Santana wiped the blood off his face as he rose up off the floor. He looked down at his former friend, a nigga that he considered his family at one point in his life. The look of Montez disgusted Santana to the core. He knew Montez would probably have to become a memory now, because one thing was for certain, he and Montez couldn't live around each other after he did him so dirty. When Montez began to wake up, he spoke.

"Clean yourself up. If you ever steal from me again or from any of my niggas, I'll blow ya face off, pussy, and I mean that with all of me!" Santana spoke firmly and he meant every word. "You hear me, nigga? I will kill you where you stand. Test me if you want, you swine ass nigga." Santana spit venom with each word that was released from his mouth. Santana wiped his gun clean from the blood that was dripping from it. He hated that he had to do Montez like that, but it was a must that it was done. He wasn't willing to tolerate no kind of disloyalty shown to him and his. He shook his head as he looked down yet again at Montez sprawled on the floor. Santana just couldn't let it go, so he spoke what was on his chest.

"Then you had the flicking nerve to take all my money. You a bitch ass nigga. I swear I should kill ya faggot ass. You know I came down here fucked up, son. You know I don't have anyone down here to look after me when shit gets real. You rather let me starve out this bitch so

you can buy yourself some clothes, my G? I thought you loved me, nigga, if that's love, pussy!" Santana wiped his face; that shit killed him inside. This was all he had left of Justice and he had just lost that. Santana trained his gun on Montez. Montez drowsily looked into the barrel of Santana's gun. Once he realized what was taking place, he began to plead for his life.

"Bruh, please, I'm sorry. I don't know what the fuck I was thinking, my nigga. Please, bruh, don't!" Montez pleaded. That whack ass pleas grabbed at Santana's heart string. He looked at Montez and saw so much of Justice in his features. To look Montez in the eyes and kill him would feel as if he was killing Justice. That's how much they resembled each other.

"Fuck you do me like that for, huh, nigga? You know I'm out this bitch fucked up. Fuck! You don't love me, son. I swear the only reason you still breathing is for the love I have for my brother. Thank Justice, you bitch ass nigga!" Santana replied and squeezed the trigger—*Boc!*—shooting Montez in his hand.

"Swine ass nigga, and you bet not tell Kat." Santana grabbed what shit he had packed prior to the event. He tucked his pistol into his waist band and walked out into the beautiful, but cold afternoon. Santana was sick about doing Montez like that, but what people didn't understand about him was that he wasn't the same little nigga that grew up on Courtland four years ago. He was a different person through and through. He was the true definition of being a product of his environment. He learned to adapt to situations quickly because he knew if he didn't he would most likely pay costly with his life. And with knowing that, he wasn't willing to play those type of games with nobody, that includes the people he called family. The only person immune to his gun was his mother, because at the end of the day she was the only person that was worthy of his trust. Everyone else, and he meant everyone else, could get it if their loyalty came into question. Anybody! He made that pledge long ago while he sat in his cell on them lonely nights in Clinton Hall. Those were the same nights that he felt all was against him, all but Simfany and Drew.

Santana hit the alley on the side of Kat's house and walked until he got to the backyard of Zach's house. He threw his bag over the fence, and then hopped across it, leaving all the bullshit behind him. He walked up to the back door and tried to open it; it was locked so he walked around to the front and knocked on the door. Zach opened the door with Moca in tow. *Damn, that dog don't do no playing when it comes to this nigga*, Santana thought happily. He wished he had someone or something that cared that much about him besides his mother. With the thoughts of seeing such loyalty, the thoughts of his mother surfaced his head. He hadn't really talked much to Simfany since he'd been in West Virginia. Being on the run for murder made a lot of shit change. He chalked it up to taking care of unwanted problems, but he promised himself when shit slowed down and he got situated, he would call to hear his mother's voice.

***

Tijuana walked out the bathroom with tears in her eyes. She was pregnant, and she didn't know by who. Before her and Santana unexpectedly made love, she had let C.O. Green hit her two weeks prior. She shook her head. *T, chill, these symptoms started after you and Santana.* She tried to persuade herself into calming down.

"What's wrong with you?" Ms. Burke's voice scared the shit out of her. Tijuana thought about lying, but that was something she wasn't used to doing, so she didn't.

"I'm pregnant!" Tijuana cried.

"And that's a bad thing?" her mother asked with a worried look on her face. Ms. Burke always thought her daughter wanted a child, especially after her oldest son was killed to gang violence. She was happy and confused all at the same time. The tears were what caught Ms. Burke off-guard. It wasn't her business, so she just followed her daughter's lead.

"Awww, ma, these are happy tears. I thought I wasn't ever going to have children." Tijuana lied, but with a little truth attached to it. Ms. Burke saw through her bullshit, but she let her have it. What she wasn't going to do was argue with her about something that she felt shouldn't be her business. Fake smiles and overbites, then that's what it would be.

"Congratulations, baby. What do you think you will have?" Ms. Burke asked. "Better yet, what would you like to have?"

"Really, momma, it doesn't even matter as long as the lor one is healthy. But if I had a say-so, I would love to be blessed with a boy. I feel like us females don't get a fair chance at life unless you're pretty and ambitious. But for a boy, the possibilities are endless. I know a lot of lames niggas that get shot after shot. They just don't ever use them to better themselves. They love this hood shit." She laughed as she wiped her tears away. Ms. Burke walked over to her daughter and hugged her tightly.

"I love you, baby."

"I love you too, momma." Mother and daughter smiled at the new growing life about to enter their family. Ms. Burke's face was of disappointment as she hid her frustrations. She promised herself whatever secrets her daughter wanted to keep were Tijuana's demons, not her own. So she let go and let Allah deal with it.

***

Santana was in Zach's room pacing back and forth. He was nervous after what happened between him and Montez. Not killing Montez was dumb on his part. He left a witness that could tell on him. He was already on the run for a body he didn't commit. He had to call his mother. Santana had to calm down, he was tripping. Zach was downstairs cooking, thankfully, while he and Moca came upstairs. He called his mother; Simfany's phone rang three times before he heard her angelic voice pick up.

"Hey, baby boy. What you been up to?" Simfany said excitedly. He could hear the music playing smoothly in the background. *She must be cleaning the house up. Is that Keith Sweat playing in the background? No, she ain't.* He could imagine her swirling around the house cleaning everything. He could even smell the Pine Sol invade his nose at that moment. He missed the good ole days when he ain't have to worry about shit but going outside to chill with his people.

"My day hasn't been as good as yours, that's for sure." Simfany paused for a second. She knew when something was bothering her only child.

"Hold on a second, lor nigga." Santana could hear the hint of Baltimore in his mother's already heavy accent. He heard the music cut off. She was definitely about to cut into him.

"So what's been going on, Santana?" she asked firmly.

"Man, look." Simfany knew it was always bullshit coming after that statement and paused. She didn't say anything just yet; she listened.

"Ain't no reason to beat around the bush. I just shot Montez in his—"

"Nigga, what!" Simfany yelled at the top of her lungs through the phone.

"Ma, hold on, let me explain. The money you gave me—" Santana tried to explain.

"I don't give a fuck what you're talking about. Why the fuck—"

Santana hung up; it was no reason to talk while she was so vexed. She was pissed to the core and he knew it. No matter what he said, he would get cursed out. He was in serious trouble, that he knew for sure. But it was what it was. He wasn't about to hear her talking all crazy to him, and all she like to do now is make excuses why somebody had to feel the wrath of her pistol. In an instance his T-Mobile Sidekick started ringing. His mother's beautiful face popped up on the screen as the caller. He sighed. *If only that's what her face looked like right now*, he thought as he answered the phone.

"Hello?"

"So that's what we doing now? You hanging the phone up on your mother?" Santana could hear the venom in her voice; he knew it would subside though. So he stayed calm.

"Ma, I didn't hang up. You tripping though, can you stop yelling at me about this bitch ass nigga? I'm serious, I'm not about to sit and listen to that shit. Not right now. That nigga didn't give a fuck about me being hungry out this bitch by my lonely self, so fuck that faggot ass nigga. I love you, ma, but you have to let me make decisions by myself. I feel he deserved it because of the theft, so regardless of your feeling of the situation, I feel justified. Shit, the only reason the bitch ass nigga still breathing is because of the love I share with Justice!" Santana ranted.

"So you over here rambling, but you're not telling me what happened. What the fuck happened, Santana?" Simfany was all ears; she wanted to hear what the bullshit was this time.

"Alright, the money you gave me I hid in the back of a brick inside of the basement in Kat's house." Simfany was pissed solely off of the fact Santana had to hide his money.

"Nigga, why would you do something so stupid? I gave you—"

"So, ma, are you going to keep cutting me off or are you going to let me talk?" Santana asked frustratingly. He continued to explain. "I loosened a brick in the basement because I stopped staying in that house. They tend to leave the door unlocked at all times of the day, even at night when the whole house is sleeping. I lock the door, they get mad; but it ain't even what this is about, just what led up to me using this hiding spot. So I put it there, I ended up meeting this old nigga and through him I met this cool ass nigga named Zach. And before you get to tripping, know I'm grown and I got me. Anyway, that much money I just can't keep on my person. That would probably get me sent to jail, so I hid it in the basement. The old head turned out to be the plug for real. I wanted to flip my money and I have, so, no money is needed by the way. Anyway, long story short, I go one night to grab some money to buy a little pack from the old head. Of course, the door is open, that's one of the reasons I left the money there, all night access. I sneak in and sneak out, or so I thought. But the instinct in me is telling me to go and look through the window that leads to the basement, and I do just that. It was to make sure I wasn't followed down there. I see Montez, but Montez doesn't see me." Simfany sighed, she knew where the story was going without the finishing touches, and by all accord it was making her mad also to hear that Montez would do that to her son; especially knowing his situation.

"But I saw his bitch ass go behind the step and wiggle the brick that my money was being held behind. He stood there and counted the money for a second. I chalked it up as the nigga being nosey. He knew what he was doing. He just watched me only seconds earlier. I didn't think much about it afterwards. I went and did my numbers and came back to see all my money was gone. This nigga didn't leave shit. He wasn't trying to hide it and take a few hundred. He took all of it.

The nigga didn't leave shit, ma, and it was a couple of bands left. I'm not sure how much exactly. So I came home and waited on this nigga. Listen to this shit, when Montez walked through the door, this nigga had the nerve to have both his hands full with shopping bags." Simfany laughed at Montez's bravery.

"That shit not funny, ma. It was like he didn't care if I knew he took my shit. So I pistol-whipped him and shot his ass in the hand. That nigga needed death. I couldn't end him though. He looks too much like Justice. I left for now. I'm at Zach's house hoping this pussy ass nigga don't tell." Simfany laughed again once he was done. She wasn't laughing at what he had done to Montez, but she laughed an eerie laugh at what she had created. Santana was a savage and only at the age of sixteen. *He just barely turned sixteen several months prior, and this nigga is already a force to be reckoned with,* she thought to herself.

"Look, baby boy, you have to chill, okay. You have to give niggaz a way out sometimes. Everyone doesn't have to be shot, Santana. Chill the fuck out and I mean it. I have all the money you will need, get out the streets now! You handled your business, so put that killing shit away and live your life, baby. I'm serious. You don't really know

anyone out there. You are wanted for murder and still you're managing to show your ass. How? Those are big red letters that scream *fall
back*. Please I don't want to see you in jail, Santana, damn it!" Simfany began to cry out of frustration. The burden of lies was weighing
on her. She still hadn't told him that she was the one who killed Jimdog and his friend. In time she would, but at this moment, that was a
dead issue.

"Promise me you will chill out?" Simfany asked through the tears.
The sound of his mother's voice tore him internally. He hated to hear
her cry.

"I got you ma, but understand that I'm not playing with these niggas at all. He supposed to be family, fuck that nigga!" Santana exclaimed.

"I'm going to call Kat to see what she thinks happened. Until then,
stay put. You hear me? I'm serious, Santana. Chill your fucking ass
out. Did I talk to you about Paris snake ass yet? I can't remember,
this sour got my mind fried." She laughed out loud. "I love you, baby
boy." She kissed him through the phone.

"I love you too, pretty lady." He returned the kiss through the
phone. Santana hung up feeling better than when he called. She
wasn't as mad as he thought she would be. Simfany was definitely
disappointed; that he could hear in her tone of voice. At the end of
the day he did what he felt needed to be done, especially to a nigga
that loyalty waivered right in front of his eyes. Santana sat his phone
down on the bed and rubbed Moca's furry coat as she laid at his feet.
*Damn, what the fuck that nigga cooking down there? That shit smell
good as fuck*, Santana thought as he flipped through the TV channels.
Santana stopped on *BET*; the station was playing a rerun marathon of
Martin. Santana kicked his shoes off and laid back into the recliner;
he was tired as hell. He hadn't really had a chance at sleep since he
bought that crack from N.O. The money was definitely worth the
sleep deprivation.

"Come here, girl. Santana patted his lap for Moca to climb aboard
and rest. Moca stood up and looked at Santana with a suspicious
frown on her face. Moca knew she couldn't make the leap, but she
tried anyway. Her old nails scraped across the floor as she continued

to try her luck with the recliner. Santana laughed at her feeble attempts, then after a second he finally helped her up on to his lap. Moca was very old in age; Zach had to have her since he was a young child.

Santana had to admit, she was one of the realest dogs that he'd ever seen. She was the epitome of being a man's best friend. After she got up on to the recliner, she spun around a few times, stretched and positioned herself comfortably on his lap. Santana caught himself spoiling Moca already; the type of love she was giving out, he was receptive to.

"Hold on, girl, I 'm sorry, let me get this before we both end up hurt." Even though she didn't understand what was being said, she acted as if she did. Santana slightly moved her to the side and took his Glock off his hip. He placed the compact pistol on the table to the right of him. He reached into his back pocket and took his bandanna out of his pocket and placed it over the gun, concealing it from plain view. Moca barely budged. Once Santana stopped moving around, she got comfortable all over again. She laid her head on his thigh and closed her eyes. She was probably worn out from waiting up all night for Zach to come home. The day was long and Santana was also exhausted. He closed his eyes and drifted into a much needed slumber.

***

"Nigga, wake the fuck up!" Kevin hit Tez-Mo, abruptly waking him out his sleep. Tez-Mo jumped up and grabbed the AK-47 assault rifle that lay across his lap. He was on tilt; he was ready to bust his chopper at any slights.

"What's poppin', Ru?" Tez-Mo asked when he realized there was no danger in sight. Kevin shuffled through the *Baltimore Sun* that was lying in the table. Tez-Mo yawned and wiped the sleep from the corners of his eyes. *This nigga tripping already, damn we need to put somebody to sleep so this lor nigga can chill the fuck out.* Tez-Mo shook his head at the nonsense.

"So what's poppin,' blood? What's this that you keep looking at?" he asked as he leaned over and read the article that was outlined for him to read:

Are All Six Murders Connected?
The bodies of Jim "Dog" Parks, Joseph "Kill Mo" Wells, Patrick
"Piru" Mayfield, Jaquan "Stacks" Taylor, Hassan "Hood Ru" Amir,
and Detective Kenny Lawson were all found slain on December 19.
The question is, what connects these murders to each other? It's quite
simple. The bodies of Jim Parks and Joseph Wells are connected
through the spent trajectory of rounds found at the scene. The ballis-
tics from the gun that was used at the murder scene of Parks and
Wells were also found in connection with the spent trajectories at the
scene of Jaquan Taylor and Patrick Mayfield. The Baltimore Police
Department and Harford County's Sheriff office has teamed up in
hopes of bringing the killer or killers to justice. These two agencies
are looking for answers in connection with the slaying of decorated
Baltimore Police Detective Kenny Lawson. What truly has the police
in awe is the eerie connection to the bullets also found lodged in the
Baltimore Police Detective. The bullets that were found inside of
Lawson were also found in the bodies of Mayfield, Taylor and Amir.
We have a person of interest in connection with the murders of Parks
and Wells. This juvenile has since fled to an unknown location. We
believe the key to solving these cases lie in the safe capture of the
juvenile. Santana Vasquez is to be taken seriously and presumed
armed and dangerous. No pictures have been given of Mr. Vasquez
at this time, but a description of the juvenile—"

Tez-Mo stopped reading the paper after he saw Santana's name in it. He shook his head. He continued to read. This account of events couldn't be true:

The bodies of Jimmy "Jim "Dog" Parks and Joseph "Kill Mo"
Wells were found early the morning of December 19 on the 2400 block
of Monument and Port. A witness stated that they had seen a black
Durango styled SUV pull up beside the white Nissan Maxima. Words
were exchanged and then gun fire plagued the city, leaving two dead
bodies in its wake. The bodies of the other four victims came later in
that same afternoon only hours later in Harford County where the
juvenile's last known address is located. The city of Baltimore is in
the state of panic. And so are the communities of Harford County.

Anyone with information in the connection to these murders is urged to call crime stoppers at 410-555-5926. You will remain anonymous."

"Nah, shorty, lor yo ain't do this. He ain't do this if that's what you're going with this."

Tez-Mo threw the paper down and looked at Kevin pace the floor back and forth.

"How not, Ru? " Kevin was tripping and Tez-Mo could see it clearly. He wanted blood, he needed blood, and they both needed someone to bleed for what was done to their lost comrades.

"I'm gone kill that lor nigga, Ru!" Kevin started to cry. "We trusted that nigga, bro, why would he do the homies like that?" Kevin was distraught.

"Calm down, shorty and listen to the facts. Santana was over here the morning they say shorty killed them two niggas. We was smoking with him at the time, nigga, you have to remember. Hood and Stacks went and picked the nigga up over him having that shoot-out in front of the Shell station." He could tell that the memory brought light into Kevin's head; whether Kev wanted to admit it out loud or not, he was right. Kevin wiped his face and began to listen more intently to what his brother was saying. It had been months since the murders took place, but he was recollecting the morning that all the confusion with Santana took place.

Tez-Mo continued. "And shorty, remember when you left right before me? Piru and Hood went to grab Tana back from his spot because the police scanner reported that they had a murder suspect for the bodies of them lor niggas on Monument Street. He was at home when the scan came in. He was over here when those bodies were dropped. They had dropped him off not even thirty minutes prior. Come on, Kev, use your head, this is the only homie we have left standing with us. Shorty on the run for bodies he couldn't have dropped. The bullets that connect the bodies are wild as fuck, I can't lie, but in order for Santana to have killed the homies, he would have to be connected to those bodies in the city, which is impossible. You were in the flesh with him, Ru, and furthermore, none of us and I mean none of us, knew where Hood lived at, especially not Santana. I don't mean to put this on no one but please let's not forget bullets found in Stacks came from three guns, one being Piru's. We don't know what happened and who did it, but what we do know is, it's war!" He picked the AK-47 off his lap and tapped the stock of the gun.

"We can't engage war on just anybody though, shorty. Especially not towards a nigga we know love us. We was there the night he tried to end Nelo. Just don't forget where our loyalties lie, before and after this blood shit. Me and you popped out the same pussy, nigga, have trust in me. Now please sit your muthafucking ass down and roll that sticky shit up. I need to ease my mind from this bullshit. And nigga, why the fuck are your eyes so muthafuckin red?" Tez-Mo got upset instantly. Kev's eyes were bloodshot and anyone who knew Kev knew it wasn't from the tears he had just shed. He sat the assault rifle to the side as he approached his younger brother. Tez-Mo looked into Kevin's eyes and got vexed at what he saw.

"I should fuck you up. You doing that cat food again, nigga?" Kevin just sat there saying nothing with a dumbfounded look on his face.

"I'ma let you have that, shorty, but one more time and I swear on Diamond, I'ma eat your plate myself and tell momma I did it. Niggas is out here with these choppas and you wanna be drowning in ya fucking sorrow. Stop playing with me, my lor nigga. Get your mind right. I love you, nigga, even if no one else will. Westside, nigga."

"All the time, Ru," Kevin replied, taking all that was said into consideration. "I love you too, my nigga, I swear on momma. I'm gone chill, bro." He couldn't deny the matter of the fact; he was high as a kite. "I be on one sometimes; that's why I need you at times." Tez-Mo had heard it all before, so that shit went in one ear and out the other. What was on his mind was the chilling facts of the case. The fact that all these bullets were connected and he couldn't understand how. Santana was connected to the victims in some way, he just wouldn't be elected a suspect out of thin air. He was connected to Jimmy Parks, Joseph Wells and/or that detective. One thing he did know for sure was that Piru, Hood, and Santana opened fire on the detective when he tried to stop them from coming out the wooded area behind Meadowood. This was some deep shit, but still he wondered how all these murders could be connected. Something wasn't right about the murders because it was a lot more he felt was missing than Santana's little ass. Parts of the story he himself knew he would never figure out, but he would play his cards how they were dealt. No matter what the outcome was, he and his choppa were ready to shed blood. He refused to go out like his homies. Tez-Mo's thoughts were interrupted when Kevin hit him to pass the freshly rolled Dutch. They were the only two left standing.

They sat and reminisced about the good times they had with Hood, Stacks, Piru and even Blaze; the good times as they knew it before they met Brian "Byrd" Parks. He was the missing connection that no one bothered to pay attention to, no one but Detective Lawson. The death of Byrd started a cycle of murder, mayhem and retaliation.

Chapter Ten

"Bruh, wake up. I made steak and eggs. Moca, come on, momma, let Tana eat something," Zach stated as he patted Moca on her butt, waking her off Santana's lap. The motion of the dog in Santana's lap made him stir. As he opened his eyes, he saw Zach holding a plate of food. *That shit smell good as shit*, Santana thought as his stomach growled from hunger.

"Nigga, I ain't 'bout to sit here and hold this damn plate all night. Fuck I look like! Betty the muthafucking maid? Grab this shit before I feed it to Moca!" he joked. Santana knocked the cobwebs off from the day's events and grabbed the plate from Zach.

"Good looking, son, a nigga was light weight starving. You came through in the clutch." That was all he could say before he dug into the plate.

"Damn, nigga. This shit. . . banging," Santana managed to get out between each bite. He was starving.

"Montez got shot earlier too, if you didn't know already. They say bruh is looking bad too. Whoever did bruh dirty, they did him good or so I hear!" Zach explained as he ate.

"Fuck that nigga!" Santana mumbled under his breath. Zach looked up from his food.

"What you over there mumbling about?"

"I said fuck that nigga. He got what he deserved. I should have shot him in his muthafucking mouth!" Santana replied. Zach figured that Santana was the one to do him dirty. He also figured it was over the money Santana had told him and N.O. about. The streets were talking hard. Montez wasn't a bum type of nigga, but the shopping spree that he had just went on raised the eyebrows of many; so the shooting came as no surprise. The city knew that a lot of bullshit came with Montez, so when he dropped a couple bands on shoes and clothes, they sat back and waited for the consequence.

I fuck with the nigga, but that was some grimy shit. To steal fiom your fam though, bruh. What were you thinking? Zach was the only one that knew where the source of the thievery came from, the rest of Charleston figured he found someone's stash in an alley and got what deserved. *News travels fast around this muthafucka,* Santana thought to himself.

"What N.O. been up to?" Santana changed the subject. Zach couldn't help but laugh at how raw Santana was.

"Getting to that money probably, that nigga definitely about his money," Zach replied. Santana understood at that moment he was the only one to know about N.O. playing his old head role. He had to constantly remind himself that not everyone was built for that gunplay shit and by just watching Zach's demeanor, he felt the nigga really wasn't built for that kind of action. Not yet at least.

Santana finished his plate, leaving nothing but the bone from the steak.

"Now that was good, my G. I appreciate that, but a nigga still hungry. I'm bout to run to Gino's and grab some chicken wings. You want me to grab you anything?" Zach looked at Santana for a second and shook his head. He was still engrossed in his own plate.

"I'm good, bruh. I don't eat much for real. I appreciate it though. As a matter of fact, grab me some *Now Later's.* Good looking, bruh," Zach replied and dug back into his food.

"I got you, son," Santana said as he picked his bandanna and gun off the table. He put his burgundy bandanna in his back pocket, nodded at Zach and walked down the stairs. When he got to the bottom, he stopped and looked up at the top of the stairs; without disappointment Moca stood there watching Santana out. Santana shook his head; he had to admit Moca was one of a kind. He smiled as he opened the door and walked into the day. Santana texted Zach as he walked down the street: *Come lock the door, my G, I'll call you when I'm on my back.* Zach texted back immediately: *I got you, bruh.* Zach would usually leave the door open until he came back, but he knew that Santana hated the thought of an open door.

Santana walked down the street looking to see if he had any missed calls. He had a lot more than he wished to have. Kat was blowing up his phone, he had a call from an unknown number and his boo—Tijuana—called. He had had been missing her like crazy, but he was into everything, so time was of the essence. Kat had called five times back to back. *That bitch ass nigga bet have not told his*

mother on me. Santana shook his head at the situation Montez put him in. He let the thought leave his head as he moved on. Tijuana had called a few times, and the unknown number he just didn't pay attention to. He made a mental note to hit Tijuana back when he settled in. He reluctantly dialed Kat's number from memory. *Kat is probably about to go*
ape shit on me. Fuck, let's get this shit over with. He thought of ways to calm her, but came up blank. He was just going to tell her some of the truth of the matter.

"Hello?" Kat answered aggressively.

"What's up? I see you been banging my phone all crazy like. You good, ma?" Santana asked nonchalantly.

"First off, where the fuck are you?"

"Whoa, ma, who you talking to like that? Please don't speak to me as if I'm your child. If you have a problem with me not being to your disposal, I apologize, but please watch your tone, no disrespect." Santana stood his ground.

"My bad, baby, I'm just trying to figure out where you been for the most part. I haven't seen you in days. You hear what happen to your cousin?" Kat asked.

"What cousin? I don't have any family out here, that was made clear," Santana said meaning every word.

"I don't know what the fuck you talking about, little nigga, but you need to get your ass home. I don't have time for Simfany being on bullshit with me." Kat ignored his initial comment. Montez must be going to the grave with what happened to him. Santana walked into
Gino's restaurant on East Washington Street.

"Hold on for a second," he told Kat. Then to the restaurant girl: "Can I get a twenty piece hot wing with extra ranch dressing and a large cheese pizza please. I'll be back; I'm going over to the bodega across the street. How much I owe you?"

"Twenty two dollars and fifty cents," the girl behind the cash register said as she wrote the order out to give the cook. Santana counted out the money he owed and handed it to the cashier.

"Thank you," Santana said politely. *Damn, this bitch bad!* he thought to himself as he walked out the door almost forgetting Kat was on the phone. He made a mental note to check shorty's temperature on his way back.

"Oh shit, hello?" Santana talked into his Sidekick.

"Yeah, I'm here," she replied with an attitude.

"My bad. I was ordering some food for me and my nigga."

"Your nigga? Boy, please you ain't been here long enough to—forget it." Kat was agitated, which was to be expected.

"I'm not going back to your house, Kat, I talked to my mom already about it. I can't do the *open door policy* shit y'all got going on. I'll stop by and show my love, but other than that, I can't lay my head there. Plus ya son got too many enemies to be safe there. I hope that can be a lesson to leaving your door open. I love you though with ya sexy ass." He teased her, trying to bring a smile to her face and lighten the situation.

"Whatever, Santana, you just make sure you come and holla at me every day so I can know that you are okay. And I don't give a fuck what you talking 'bout, don't make me come looking for you. I love your high yellow ass too. Niyah been asking about you. In all truth the fam has missed you. Stop by later when we come from General with Montez stupid ass. Man, this stupid ass nigga, stealing somebody shit like that. Damn! I love you, Tana, hit me later."

"I got you, ma, I'll slide in later on. I promise you," Santana said, thinking Kat wouldn't catch the jab he just threw her way.

"This ain't what you want, little boy, your ass really won't be running the streets then," Kat replied seductively, and then hung up. Santana smiled at Kat's crazy ass comment as he waited on the traffic to cross the street. He looked across the street to the familiar face: N.O. was outside the Shop n Go all dressed up begging for money. *This nigga serious, he don't be playing. He want blood*! Santana thought as he approached and tipped his hat. Santana walked into the store with a smile on his face, shaking his head. He was so lost in his own thoughts he didn't notice the fat dude standing to the right of the store or the man hanging by the pay phone on the corner of the store front. Santana went and grabbed Zach every flavor of *Now & Later* they had on the shelf and two Long Island Iced Teas out the cooler. He walked to the cashier and paid for his groceries. He looked out the window as he paid and saw nothing out of place. The scene that would take place would forever be etched in his memory.

***

Simfany was woken from her day dream when her phone began to ring loudly. It seemed as if her phone was ringing louder than ever before. She picked the phone up and looked at the caller ID. It was Kat calling. The picture that showed every time Kat called broke her heart. It was a picture of her, Kat and Lonnie as teenagers standing in front of *IS 183*. Simfany loved that picture dearly; it reminded her of the innoence that they once shared. Simfany didn't want to dodge her longtime friend, but Kat be on bullshit nowadays.

"Hey, pussy Kat?" Simfany answered reluctantly.

"Hey, momma," Kat replied.

"What you been up to?" Simfany fished; she didn't know if she knew that Santana was responsible for her son being shot or not.

"At the hospital with Montez dumb ass. He did some dumb shit to somebody and got himself shot in the hand. They beat that nigga ass kind of good too. Poor baby. I'm all cried out, been crying all day over this nigga. He won't tell me shit like I'm the fucking police, but you know the streets talk. The streets are saying that Montez stole somebody's shit out of an alley or something similar, and then went shopping with the money. He gets that shit from his broke ass daddy because I don't get down like that, though that wasn't the reason I called. I'm calling about Mr. Vasquez grown ass." Simfany sighed. *Here we go*, Simfany thought to herself.

"Man, what Santana do now?" she asked curiously. Knowing Santana, he was always getting into some shit. If Kat knew that Santana shot Montez, Kat would have brought it up already. So what she was about to say was a different situation altogether.

"He hasn't done anything dumb yet, but he said that he had talked to you about staying somewhere else. That true?" Kat asked, confused.

"Ohhhh, yeah, I did tell him if he didn't feel comfortable he could buy his own spot. He told me that y'all be leaving the door unlocked all the time. He has enough money to buy himself a one bedroom if that's what he wants to do. I don't know how y'all handle that out there. I do apologize though. I been meaning to call you about this, I just been busy getting my kitty cat purred." Simfany lied, kind of.

"Do tell." Kat got excited with her nympho ass.

"Girl, watch out; I don't kiss and tell. This you know. I actually have to get to my fun, if you don't mind, love. Call me back and you bet not say shit to Santana bad ass. Love you, girl."

"Ummm huh, love you too, chula. Muah! Call me."

"Muah." Simfany kissed back. "Got you, mommy." Simfany hit the end button, laughing at her longtime friend. She wasn't lying when she said that she was getting her kitty cat purred; it just wasn't by no man or woman. What made her pussy wetter nowadays was busting that tool of hers. She was in the middle of reading the *Baltimore Sun* before she began to wonder off in thought. Simfany had made sure that the article was real and not part of her day dreaming. She picked the paper up and there it was, an article of Detective Ramos giving a statement on the connection between each murder. The forensic team in Maryland was impeccable. She shook her head; the article named one suspect to the crimes, her only child Santana Vasquez. To the police he was the only connection to the murders at one site, the others they had no real leads, but the bullets that were found lodged and examined in the victims matched; that's what made the murders a big deal. The guns were long gone, so any chances of them finding the twin Glocks were far to none. What stood out as the focal point to the cases was the murder of Detective Lawson. Santana hadn't spoken on that with her yet, but she made a mental note to inquire about it. At the end of the day she couldn't feel any type of way because she still hadn't told Santana she was the one that killed Jim Dog and his homie. In due time she would, or so she kept telling herself. Damn, it's crazy they connected all these bodies. *Detective Ramos, you good, but it is no way you that good.* She tried to laugh it off.

If only she knew how far in deep she was herself, she would steer clear and play under the trenches and wait for the smoke to clear; even if it took years. This was life in prison with the possibility of the death penalty. The only thing that gave her comfort was the fact that her name wasn't plastered all over the news wanted for murder. She felt that because the news or TV didn't announce her she was safe from prosecution, and in all reality she was; for the moment.

With the information that Ramos held dear to him, all parties involved were bound to die in prison. Simfany knew at the end of it all, if she slipped, it would be someone there to catch her.

***

It was something about the man's eyes that had Santana on edge when he walked out of the store. The scenery was all wrong, or it felt as if it was at least. He always followed his gut feelings. Santana walked over to his old head, bent down and gave him some money as a ploy to say what was on his mental.

"Old head, watch the nigga on the corner near the phone behind me. He doing too much. But I could just be paranoid. I rather you be on point though." Santana informed N.O. as discreetly as possible.

"I got'em, souljah. I can't place the face, never seen the youngin' before. He a new face, but . . ." *Boc—Boc—Boc—* Santana grabbed for the left side of his stomach. The bullets that pierced his back ripped through the front of his abdomen. His eyes grew wide and his mouth crunched up from the flame of each shell that hit him. N.O. pulled Santana to the ground and opened fire from under his dingy clothing. *Boc—Boc—Boc—Boc—Boc—* N.O. shot aimlessly behind Santana, hoping to back the reaper off his little man. The bullets sparked off the pay phone that sat on the corner of the store front. N.O. laid Santana to the side, trying to protect him from any more possible wounds. Santana wasn't into wasting time on being stagnant; he reached into his waist line and pulled his Glock out and raised it toward the last place he knew the shooter to be. Santana felt like he was being held captive because of the small space and air he was allowed to breath. He panicked.

"Nigga, get off me! Where that nigga at?" Santana tried to move again, but the pain from his wounds hindered his movement.

"I'm good! We have to kill this nigga, son!" Santana yelled with what strength he had left. The pain that was beginning to spread through his body was almost becoming unbearable. Santana looked into N.O.'s eyes as a bullet pierced his skull, splattering brain matter and blood onto his face. *Boc—Boc—Boc—Boc—* the shots went wild missing Santana altogether. Santana had no time to think; his reaction went without thought. It was 'kill or be killed'. Santana fired at the figure that looked down on him gun in hand. *Boc— Boc— Boc—* He saw the mist of blood explode with each shot. The man staggered back as if he was punched. The power of the impact threatened to sit him on his ass. Catching his balance, he raised his gun and fired, hitting Santana in his chest cavity. The bullets' impact took Santana's breath; he knew it wasn't the time to feel pain. Both men fired in hopes of surviving the deadly encounter. Santana heard the sirens in the distance as he continued to fire. He hadn't felt any more bullets pierce his body, and the Glock indicated that he had no more bullets left to give. He looked at his gun's slider in disbelief. He knew it was over. *Damn, blood* was all he thought to himself. Santana looked around, trying to find the threat. He rose up off the ground to see the man slumped on the side of the store in the alley in a convulsive state. Santana instinctively grabbed for N.O. but was met with a vision that would forever stay with him, half of N.O.'s face was swollen and missing from the bullet that entered and exited his skull.

"Fuck—Fuck—Fuck!" Santana yelled. He had to think quickly. The sirens were getting closer and closer. He pushed off of N.O.'s body to get away and saw his gun lying there with blood covering it. He grabbed the gun with N.O.'s dingy clothing and wiped his finger prints off. Santana stuck the gun into N.O.'s hand, not caring how the police found the scene. Three guns, two people dead, it would raise questions for sure. He didn't care about none of that at the moment; he needed to get gone, and he needed to do it fast. Santana ran his comrade's pockets, he found what he was looking for—the keys to N.O.'s Buick. He also took the money that was there. Santana ran slowly; he was badly wounded. The blood dripped from his wounds as he stood to his best ability. Santana stumbled through the alley way past the grim reaper; he coughed. He felt his mouth fill up with liquid.

He spit the blood out his mouth and continued to move in search of his friend's car. Each step that Santana took weakened him. Santana was losing blood rapidly. The wound in his chest and abdomen was proving to be life-threatening. From previous occasions he knew where N.O. parked his Buick. Santana's only thought was to get as far away from the murder scene as possible. He was going in and out as he stumbled to the parked car. *Nigga, wake the fuck up*, he coached himself to stay alert. Santana had an urge to go to sleep, but he knew if he went out, he may never wake up again. So he was determined to get some kind of help before it was too late.

Santana finally made it to the Buick and put the key into the ignition, but he was way too weak to turn the key. He didn't have a clue how to drive any way; he was all fucked up. This was a life-or-death matter; so it was an absolute must that he got his shit together, or the life that he once knew and loved would be over. The thought of being a mere memory sparked an idea, an idea that could possibly save his life. Zach . . . Santana reached into his pocket and pulled his phone out with what strength he had remaining.

"Fuck!" he moaned as he dialed Zach's number. "Arrrrraaaagggggghhhhhhhh!" Santana winced in pain from the movement. Luckily, Zach answered the phone on the first ring.

"Bruh, you out there shooting?" Zach joked. He knew Santana was a fire cracker. Santana smiled. He tried to respond but coughed up blood again.

"Son, I'm 'bout to die. Come—help—me—Shop N Go—N.O. dead—" Santana coughed up what felt like fire. "Help—me—bro—" Santana began to cry out of frustration. He could hear Zach running on the other end of the line. It was one more call that needed to be made before he met his maker. He pressed 1 to speed dial his mother. Simfany answered energetically.

"Hello, baby boy. What's the pleasure, twice in one day? Okay, now I feel loved."

Santana smiled at his mother's angelic voice. "Ma, I—I love—love you. I swear you are my only true love. I—" Santana cried at the possibility of not ever being able to see his mother again. Simfany could hear the hurt in Santana and instantly began to panic. She had never heard him sound like that before.

"Baby, what are you talking about?" Simfany asked, concern etched in her soul.

"I'm leaking out, I . . . I got . . . lacking, ma. I love you, pretty lady," Santana said in a whisper.

"What the fuck? My nigga, what the fuck happened?" Zach opened the driver side door, out of breath.

"Shot— G—S—R—" Santana saw Zach and knew he couldn't fight the sleep no longer. He closed his eyes and finally succumbed to the terror of his possible death.

"Santana!" Simfany yelled through the phone.

"Wake up, bruh, I have to move you." While trying to move him, the thought had finally hit him about what he meant about the GSR, Zach took his shirt off and hopped out the car. He forced the piss out of his body. He pissed on his shirt until it was wet. He wiped Santana's arms, face, hands and clothes.

"Sorry, bruh." Zach apologized for wiping his urine on his body. Simfany heard Zach's voice through her end of the phone.

"Hello!" Simfany yelled as she cried hysterically.

"Hold on!" Zach yelled back. "I have to get Tana out the driver's seat, man, fuck it. We don't have time for this." Zach pushed the seat all the way back and took a seat on the edge of the seat between Santana's legs. He started the ignition and sped down Lee Street until he got to the intersection of CAMC hospital. Zach ran the light and parked the Buick on the front curb of the emergency room. Zach got out the car and picked Santana up, almost dropping him. The dead weight wasn't a good sign and the loss of blood began to scare him. He was finally able to secure Santana over his shoulder and ran into the hospital screaming for help.

"Help! I—I need a doctor now!" Zach yelled at the top of his lungs, capturing the attention of everyone in an ear shot radius of the lobby. Zach laid Santana on the floor and before he was able to yell yet again, he looked up into the worried eyes of Kat, Santana's aunt. Kat had just left the cafeteria as Zach ran into the hospital. She had heard the yelling and whispering so she came to find out what was going on. Not in a million years could she be prepared for the sight she saw. Kat looked at a bloody Santana, took a step back and fainted. The commotion in the lobby grabbed the curiosity of Raven also, she looked around and saw that her mother was laid out on the floor. Filled with confusion, she looked around to see what the fuck was going on. When she looked past her mother and saw Santana bleeding from his head to his waist, she ran over there to his aide.

"Baby, please wake up—please wake up, baby!" Raven cried hysterically. She laid on the ground so she could be leveled with him. Raven stroked his head and ran her through his hair.

"Baby, please wake up—Please!" Santana stirred, but didn't open his eyes. Zach looked at Santana just lying on the ground covered in blood. The feeling of loss was mounting. Zach silently cried tears for his friend as a swarm of doctors and nurses took Santana away on a gurney.

"I'll be back, let me go handle something real quick," Zach told Raven as he helped her off the ground and into a chair next to a shaken Kat. Kat was out it; but she had regained consciousness. The sight of Santana caused hysteria for them all. Kat thought of her best friend and soulmate, Simfany. What words would she be able to render? Simfany had trusted her with the well-being of her only child. Kat felt the only thing that could keep her alive was Santana surviving. If he died, she knew that most likely her fate would be the same, no matter how long they had been friends.

Zach ran out the exit and hopped in N.O.'s car; he pulled off in a hurry. He wanted to hurry up and get back inside. He pulled the car around back to the parking lot and parked the Buick in the nearest parking spot, but still out of plain sight. Zach grabbed Santana's T-Mobile Sidekick off the floor of the car. The phone was covered in blood, as was the seat and steering column. Zach searched the car for any kind of evidence that connect Santana to the bodies laid on the pavement in front of the Shop n Go. When none was found, he locked the car up and ran back into the hospital. There he would sit and wait for the news regarding Santana's fate.

***

Simfany cried. She couldn't understand anything that was happening. Santana sounded badly hurt and the boy on the other end of the phone sounded as if he had tears in his throat as well. Simfany called Santana's phone repeatedly, getting no answer. Before she could call again her phone rang. She recognized the number as Santana's, she answered the phone immediately.

"Baby, what's going on?" she asked hysterically.

"Who is this?" the voice on the phone belonged to someone other than Santana. That sunk Simfany's heart.

"Who the fuck is this and what the fuck happened to my son?" Simfany screamed through the phone. Zach was on the other end; the pain he heard in her voice began to break his heart more and more. Simfany heard the caller get quiet; she didn't want whoever it was to hang up so she took a different approach. She changed her speech and tone.

"Please tell me what is going on. I'm getting scared. Please tell me what happened to my son." She begged; the tough shell was now gone. She needed to know if her baby was going to be okay.

"This is Zach. Santana was shot multiple times, but I'm not sure how many times. All I know is Tana went out to get some pizza and wings, like ten minutes later I heard gunshots then received a call from Santana telling me to come and get him." The thought of her son going through the same pain that she once felt sent daggers through her soul. Zach continued.

"So I ran to find him, and that's when I came over the phone while y'all were talking. I couldn't really talk then because I had to try and move bruh out the way of the driver's seat so I could drive to the hospital. Luckily for him, the hospital was only a block away, getting him there was the most important thing at the time. I'm sorry for ignoring you, ma'am. Kat passed out, and Raven seems like she lost it. I'm the only one keeping us together. I'll be here when you get here. I'm not going home until you get here. You are coming, right?" Zach asked, knowing the question was a stupid one.

"I'm on my way now. Thank you for saving my baby's life, Zach. We owe you for that. That's if he makes it." Simfany sniffled away the oncoming tears.

"Ma, bruh going to make it, God got him. Have faith and all will be well." Those were the words she wasn't trying to hear; because if it was up to God right now, Santana would be a lost soul drifting into to the abyss. God wasn't quite happy with them two right now.

"I'll call you as soon as I make it in ya city. I'm leaving now," Simfany assured Zach.

"Okay, just hit me and I'll come and meet you," Zach replied and hung up.

Jamel Mitchell

Chapter Eleven

Simfany pulled into the hospital later that night. She kept in contact with Zach and Kat on her entire way up the interstate. The updates were the same, no news. But how Simfany looked at it, if he had survived this long then he should be okay. Plus she knew that her baby was a fighter. She still prayed for him. Simfany drove around the parking lot until she found a spot that was suitable for her. She parked then called Zach.

"Hello?" Zach answered with his country style accent.

"What's up? I'm outside of the hospital. Has there been any new news?" Simfany asked as she sparked a blunt and inhaled deeply.

"Actually, yeah, he came out of his surgery and now is being placed into a ICU room. Tana gone be good. As far as I know, they aren't letting no one come back there yet," Zach said hopelessly.

"A'ight, come outside so we can go eat and then see him."

"Okay," Zach replied, then hung up. Simfany sat in her car for a minute with her own thoughts and a blunt. *Everywhere this nigga go he gone cause hell. This nigga did this shit in broad fucking day. This wild wild west shit gone get this nigga forever in prison. I'm not trying to lose my son again. God, please I'm begging for your help with him.* She looked into the sky for support. One thing she couldn't do was blame nobody but herself for the savage in him. She was for sure to blame. She finally realized that she might have created a monster. Her thoughts were cut short as Zach opened the door to her all-black on black Tahoe. Instinctively, Simfany reached for the Glock .21 she had resting in the middle console and trained it on Zach's face.

"And you are?" Simfany questioned without putting the gun down. The blunt still hanging from her pretty lips. The look of the unknown was stuck on Zach's face.

"Z-Z-Z . . . Zachariyah," he replied shook to death. Simfany nonchalantly placed her gun back in its resting space and pulled on her blunt.

"My bad, baby, I had to make sure that I was safe. You look young but you don't look like a kid. Get in." Simfany exhaled, blowing smoke all through her car. Simfany put the car in gear. Zach just stood there stuck on stupid.

"Nigga, get in." Simfany brought Zach out of his momentary stare. She didn't know if he was staring at her or if he was just in shock.

"Shit, my bad, Ms. Simfany," Zach said as he hopped in the truck.

"My fault, shorty, for backing out on you. I should have asked what you looked like but I pulled up. How did you know what kind of car I was in anyway?" Simfany asked as she passed him the blunt of loud. Zach looked at her and hesitated. *Fuck it*! he thought and grabbed the blunt. After what took place the entire day, he needed something to relax his soul.

"I seen ya lights on and you had Maryland tags. I tried to put two and two together," Zach explained.

"What? Santana told you he came from Maryland?" Simfany asked suspiciously.

"Nah, but bruh sound like a Baltimore nigga. He say his two's or anything with ohh in it funny as hell." He laughed

"It's a Baltimore dude out here and they damn near sound the same. I'm a street nigga, I'm cautious about who I surround myself and my people with. I fuck with Tana and after today I know I've grown to love bruh. No homo, as bruh would say. Ya son a real nigga through and through." Zach coughed as the loud tickled his lungs. Simfany hit him on the back to help stop him from choking.

"Damn, that's some good shit, Ms. Simfany," Zach said in between coughs. Simfany rolled her eyes.

"Can you please stop with the Ms. Simfany shit. And do you know how to drive?" Simfany asked as she leaned against the driver side door and looked at him one brow raised. She was baked out her mind. Simfany wanted to try to keep the image of Santana being hurt out her
mind as much as possible.

"Yeah, I'm nice behind the steering wheel for real. Why? What's up? You too high to drive?" He laughed.

"Nah, shorty, but this your city, so why not let you whip. I'm legal, ain't shit to really worry about but a ticket." Simfany shrugged and opened her door. The winter air was brisk, but nowhere near as bad as the air in Maryland or New York. They switched spots as Zach took her place behind the wheel.

"So what you want me to do now?" Zach questioned.

"I'm starving. Take me somewhere to get some food besides McDonald's or Burger King. No Chinese neither. Like I said, you got the floor. Food on me. Where do you usually eat?"

"It's a place called Gino's. It's like a pizzeria, but they sell a lot of different type of shit. Their wings are the best for real. That nigga Tana love them damn wings. As a matter of fact, he was there right before that shit happened. The shooting took place right across the street from Gino's. I can take you and show you where lil' bruh got shot, that's up to you though!" Zach said as he pulled out of the parking lot of the hospital.

"Shit, why not! My lil' nigga still here. I'm good now. I was fucked up earlier for sure because of how he called me, but knowing that he made it out of surgery calms my soul. That chicken do sound good right now too. Do they make that shit crispy or if you ask will they fry it as long as you like?" Simfany was high and hungry; her high was getting the best of her. Zach just laughed as he drove the block or so to Gino's restaurant. Zach's own thoughts had him floating in bliss that he barely was able to answer Simfany's questions. Zach pulled into the parking lot of Gino's. They both looked across the street at the yellow tape that was still roped around the gas pumps and store front. The bodies and lost souls of the two men were long gone but the candles and stuffed animals were a reminder of the tragedy of
what happened only hours earlier. The crowd of onlookers and people of broken hearts still lingered around lost.

As Simfany sighed knowing the feeling all too well, Zach spoke up trying to explain what took place earlier that day.

"This what they said happen—Tana came out the store and walked to that corner right over there." Zach pointed to the left of the store near a cut that led behind the store and into another cut.

Zach continued. "That's where this old head we knew—well, the old head we thought we knew. It was one of the homies playing as a homeless bum to bum some niggas he was having an issue with. This beef was some shit that was supposed to take place a long time ago. Shit, that nigga fooled me. I thought the bum was really a bum. Simf, that nigga was out there faithfully, rain, sleet and snow. Tana, I guess, figured it out and those niggas linked. The nigga name was N.O. He was the one that introduced me and your son to each other. So they said as Santana goes to give N.O. a beer like he always ask for, he turned and looked at the shooter that was posted on that corner near the phone." Zach pointed to the pay phone where the shooter was posted.

"I'm guessing that the shooter felt like Santana was exposing his play, which was probably right, so he fired, hitting Santana in the back. They say N.O. pulled Santana to the ground and fired on the shooter. But the nigga tricked them and came around the back near that cut over there." Zach pointed to the cut that led behind the store.

"The shooter fired and hit N.O. in the head. This is where the story gets tricky—some say that they both squeeze off final shots ending dude's life. Then it's a story that Santana got hit again, then raised his gun and killed dude. I don't really know what story at this part is truth or fabrication, but after that, Santana ran N.O.'s pocket and found his keys, left his gun and went to find the Buick. That's when I got the call to come pick bro up because he was shot. That's when I'm guessing that he called you or vice versa. I'm not sure and at this point it doesn't matter. I got Tana to the hospital. I don't know how the police looking at it. They might look at it as he was caught in the middle of a war that had nothing to do with him. I took his shirt and pissed on his arms and hands. I know that sounds nasty but—" Simfany cut him off.

"I know the acid from your piss cleans away gun powder residue. But how do you know?" Simfany didn't know if she was dealing with a killer, a shooter or just a kid.

"Santana told me to while I was driving him to the hospital. He made sure that I did that first before taking him inside. You knew where I learned that at, didn't you?" Zach looked over at Simfany and smiled.

"Maybe, that little nigga think he too smart, he too damn smart for his own good. Was he alert when you brought him here?"

"I wouldn't say he was alert, but I would say he was barely managing. He also wanted me to let you know that he gave them Justice's name. Whatever that meant. Other than that, here we are. Oh and I think his crazy ass shot Montez too, but that's between me and you. I never told you that and haven't said that to anyone one else. Bruh is a motherfucker man. He definitely showing me some shit that a nigga never seen or been a part of before." Zach shut up; he realized he was talking too much as is. He was high as fuck.

As Simfany looked across the street at the murder scene, Zach stole glances at her. She was too beautiful to be a nigga's mother, especially with a child his age. Her skin was radiant, her ass was phat, her titties sat perfect and her body weight, shape and glow had him on tip. To hold that type of swag and pose was ill all in the same manner. Overall, she was beautiful and dangerous and he saw that out right. It was something about mother and son that Zach didn't understand, or even fathom to understand. He was just going to go with the flow. He was caught up in his own thoughts that he lost himself yet again.

"Zach, is my ass phat?" Simfany laughed as he stared at her; he was really lost for words.

"Huh, what— nah, you tripping. Why you ask that?" Zach turned red from embarrassment.

"Nigga, I watched you stare at me for a few minutes now licking ya lips," Simfany said in a matter-of-fact tone of voice.

"Nah, I was gone right then, day dreaming 'bout some shit. I'm high as hell. That's all." Zach was so embarrassed. He hoped she didn't tell Santana wild ass about this shit. He laughed at himself for being so thirsty and getting caught.

"You good though. Niggas do it all day. That let a bitch know she still got it. Now let's go eat, fuck that crime scene they didn't chalk mines over there," Simfany said viciously as she opened the door to the restaurant. Zach shook his head from side to side and followed. *I see why Santana so wild. His mother worse than him.*

"Good evening, welcome to Gino's," the cashier said as Simfany walked to the counter and began looking at the menu.

"What's good, Darla? Ain't seen ya sexy ass in a minute. How you been holding?" Zach asked as he walked up to the counter and hugged her.

"I ain't doing shit, just working trying to make a legal check. I seen that lil' nigga that you been mobbing with get shot earlier. Is he okay? Bruhhhhh, that shit was crazy. As a matter fact he ordered some food earlier but never came back for it. I told my boss I would drop it off at the hospital when I left because he paid for his food. I know all they might do is throw it away, but so what! He still paid. I'll let the hospital throw it away if they like."

"Where ya boss at?" Simfany asked. Darla looked over at Simfany and replied.

"He left for the night, would you like to talk to someone in charge?"

"Nah, I was just curious. You got a family at home, sweetheart? That's if you don't mind me asking." Simfany leaned against the counter and looked Darla in her eyes, waiting on an answer. Darla was for sure intimidated by Simfany's assertiveness. It made Zach laugh.

"Yeah, I got a son that's a damn mess. My momma be all over and I have a younger sister. We a little dysfunctional, but we cool for the most part. We all we got, so we make it work," Darla said with love behind her words.

"Okay. Okay. I asked because I like ya grind as a single mother. I know all too much what that feels like. But to be honest, I don't know what the struggle feels like, thanks to my baby dad. I know not everyone is fortunate enough to have a nigga stick around. But more less I asked because the lor nigga you seen get shot earlier is my son, and I'm pretty sure that would be enough to grab that food, right?" Simfany shrugged.

"Yeah, technically I would think so. I was about to give it to Zach anyway."

"Nah, this what I want you to do. Take that food Santana bought and feed your family tonight. And are you allowed personal tips?" Darla shook her head by way of saying no.

"Okay." Simfany looked back up towards the menu.

"Let me get fifty crispy wings with ten packets of Ranch dressing and a sweet tea. What you want, Zach?" Simfany asked. The look Zach gave her made all of them laugh.

"What? Why you looking like that?" Simfany laughed.

"You gone crush those fifty by yourself?" Simfany burst out laughing.

"No nigga, I'm just saying if you got the munchies and you want more than that, order more. I'm just trying to eat something crispy and meaty so hurry up with ya order a bitch starving." Simfany left the pair at the counter in seek of a table to sit at.

"A'ight, Darla, give us three large sweet teas, those fifty wings and a small chicken cheese pizza."

"That'll be $53.75," Darla said as she called the order to the back.

"Zach, come here real quick." Zach walked to Simfany.

"What's good?" Zach asked curiously. It was a new surprise every time she talked. Simfany was off the chain. But only if he really knew.

"Here, take this for the food and tell girlie to bring the food to us and I'll give her a tip on the side." Simfany pulled a $100 bill from her hand purse and handed it to Zach. Zach passed the message, paid for their food and came back to the table and sat down.

"Zach, all jokes aside, I really appreciate you getting my baby to the hospital and getting him together. I'm in debt to you for the loyalty. I know you may think I'm wild and assertive. I hear that all the time. I have no filter but I try to remain that way because it's better than being angry and aggressive. You feel me? Because I can get on that bullshit. My only child is laid in a hospital with bullet holes in his body. You know how he reacted when I got shot? He showed his ass. Ya best friend is a demon. In all sense of the word. So for him to befriend you, it tells me a lot about you. Anyway, I feel like I've cried enough on my drive up here. Can't see me sweat, fear is a weakness that I pride myself to never show. Even if I feel it. I love you like my own and will flip one of these niggaz for you if ever needed. So don't . . ." Simfany cut her words short when she saw Darla walking up the aisle.

"Damn, those smell good than a muthafucka!" Simfany exclaimed as Darla sat the tray down on the table. She came back this time with the pizza and sweet teas.

"Thank you, sis." Zach said as he took a bit of one of the wings. He switched the chicken back and forth from one side to the other; it was hot.

"That's what ya greedy ass get, boy." Darla laughed, and Simfany followed suit at Zach's stupidity. Simfany reached her hand under the table all at the same time and handed Darla the money. Darla grabbed the bills and tucked them.

"Thank you for the tip and the food. I am extremely grateful." Darla damn near had tears in her eyes.

"Momma, you are welcome. As I said, I salute you, beautiful. Look at you, light-skinned, hazel eyes, a beautiful smile, your personality is awesome and you bad as hell! You go, girl. You not out here chasing these lor niggaz around to take care of you and yours. I respect that in more ways than one. I hope that helps you temporarily with ya minor setbacks. Continue to hold it down, ma, I'm rooting for you!" Simfany said with a smile of gratitude on her face. She winked then picked up a crispy thigh and began to eat. Darla nodded. Simfany gave her a nod in return.

"Thank you, what is your name?" Darla asked before walked away.

"Are you going to keep it between us?" Simfany asked as she digested her food and took a sip of tea.

"Yeah, I can do that." Darla smiled.

"My name is Simfany."

"Awww that's pretty as fuck, thank you, Simfany for the tip and the food. You are greatly appreciated. If you need anything else please let me know."

"Got you, Chula." Darla smiled and blew a kiss before she walked away. The money in her palm was burning a hole in her hand. Darla was hoping that she gave her the change left from the $100 bill she broke. Darla took off her apron and walked to the bathroom. As soon as she closed the door and locked it, she opened her palm. The crisp $100 bills almost made her faint. Simfany had given her the $46 change and four $100 bills. She tucked the money in her bra, washed her hands and exited the bathroom. She thanked God for the blessing and walked out into the dining area. Simfany and Darla made eye contact. Simfany winked at her and mouthed:

"You go, girl". Darla mouthed back a *thank you* before she returned to work. Simfany and Zach finished their food and went back to the hospital to check on Santana's condition.

***

Simfany walked into the ICU room that held Santana. He was wide awake, bringing a smile to her face. She walked closer to him. She wanted to look down into his eyes. She had missed so much; seeing him laid up in his hospital bed was crushing her soul. Simfany ran her fingers through his hair and scratched his scalp. Just how he liked when he was just a kid. Tears began to roll down her face; Simfany couldn't take the thought of losing him. She was all he had and vice versa.

"Ma . . ." Santana coughed a deep cough. His face scrunched, giving tell tale signs of pain.

"Ma—please don't cry. I just got shot a few times." He laughed. The pain in his face was evident.

"The doctor said it really didn't do too much damage. I'm gone be okay. I was told they only have me in ICU because its protocol." Santana wiped his mother's tears away. Simfany smiled. Dracula showed so much in Santana. His love, loyalty, and hard head was all the product of Cartez Vega.

"Boy, you scared me calling like that. You already know how I'm coming for you. You know I got some stupid shit sitting in the Tahoe. Plus I got Los on board for the foolery. So . . ." She let her words trail off. Santana knew all too well how long Carlos arms could reach, but Santana felt he didn't need no extended hands. After all was said and done, he always felt that Carlos was the beginning of the war anyway. He was the reason behind everybody trying to kill each other, which eventually brought Simfany into the crossfire. Carlos had definitely redeemed himself for sure. Santana was stubborn and stuck in his ways, so he steered clear of the whole Carlos situation.

"I'm good now; I thought I was going to die, and just in case I did, I wanted you to know what was going on. And that I loved you. I was able to give my love, but anything after that was impossible." Santana stuck his tongue out, trying to show his mother that all was well.

"Yeah, I hear that. So what happened?" Simfany closed the curtain to the small room and sat down. Santana explained play by play what happened leading up to the death of the two men and himself being shot in the middle of it.

"Did the detectives come question you yet?" Simfany asked cautiously as she looked around the small room. She didn't know who or what could be heard between the thin fabric of the sheet.

"Nah, no one came yet, but you know like I do they will be here soon. Did Zach tell you what I had him do?" Santana laughed.

"No, what you do to that boy?" Simfany smiled, knowing that what he was about to say was silly as hell.

"Man, that nigga refused, he so green to this street shit. I had him take my shirt and wipe me down for GSR while they rushed me into the hospital. I fuck with that nigga, he saved my life for real. Overall, he is a good nigga, no killer in him at all. But you never know what a nigga can become in a time of survival."

"Yeah, he cool, I just finished eating and smoking with him. We ate at Gino's. Ohhhh, aye, do you know the pretty little chick that work there named Darla?" Simfany asked eye brow raised.

"Nah, I don't know her. Why? She say some bullshit or something?" Santana had no clue who his mother was talking about.

"Nah, the little girl just beautiful as hell. I could never seen nothing like that dropping chicken in a basket. She cold-blooded for real. Anyway, did them bullets hit anything that can give you trouble further into your life?"

"The doctor said I should be fine and recover. Of course, I'm fucked up now but in due time with the right care, I should bounce back. I'm going to have a nice little hole in my stomach from the exit wound. The hole in my chest plate should heal right too. Other than that, I hope to recover good. These white people only tell you some of what you need to know." Santana shrugged, bringing pain into his abdomen.

"Fuck!" Santana flinched. The tears in his eyes welled up unintentionally. The pain at times was unbearable.

"Damn, this shit ain't no joke. I can only imagine what type of pain you went through after you came home from the hospital. How did you manage to recover from it mentally and physically?" Santana looked up into his mother's eyes. The pain was etched all on his face, but he acted as if he was okay.

"Vasquez's are soldiers, lor nigga. We breed and bleed differently," Simfany replied with a slight Baltimore accent. The look Santana gave her made her laugh. He was looking at her like she was damn crazy. *Man, this lady done lost her damn marbles, this shit hurt—Very bad.*

"I'm just playing, boy. Don' be looking at me like that. Time heals all wounds that ain't fatal. I just had to take it day by day. You will be okay. The hardest part passed. We're fighters, Tana, it wasn't shit with ya scary ass." Simfany joked. They both looked simultaneously as they heard the curtain being pulled back. An African man with a white lab coat walked into the room carrying a chart.

"Good evening, I'm Doctor Patrick Gwen. I'm Justice's doctor, and you are?" Doctor Gwen asked.

"His mother . . ."

"Name please?"

"Lonnie Torres. Is my son going to make a full recovery?"

"Absolutely, he should feel sore for the first two weeks due to the trauma that his body has suffered. Depending on his response to the medicine and a few tests, he should be out of ICU in the next day or so. He seems to be a very strong child mentally, and emotionally. Other than this setback, he will be able to resume regular activities in a month or two." Doctor Gwen looked over the chart, wrote a few things down. He walked over to the morphine drip hanging from him IV .

"Justice, how is your abdomen feeling? Any constant pressure? Irritation?" The doctor walked over to him and moved the bedding. He moved his gown to examine the wounds one by one. It was the worst feeling he had ever felt, but he had to bite down and sucked it up. Santana needed to get out the hospital as soon as possible.

"Ahhh, fuck!" The pain was real. The peeling of the tape hurt more than anything else.

"Sorry, sir, but of course, if you want to get better and heal it must be done." Doctor Gwen apologized as he pulled the bandage the rest of the way. He examined the wound that tunneled through Santana. He felt around the wound to see if anything was out of order or infected. When the doctor was satisfied with what he saw, he changed his gloves, then changed Santana's dressing.

"Young man, every time I look at this wound, I think how blessed you are to still be alive. Be careful, Mr. Torres, you might just have used one of your nine lives." The doctor smiled and nodded at Simfany.

"Good evening, Ms. Torres."

"Thank you, Mr. Gwen, and thank you for saving my child's life," Simfany replied gratefully.

"It's my job, ma'am." Doctor Gwen left to continue his rounds. Simfany could only imagine the type of things that doctor had seen and lived through on a daily basis.

Simfany turned and looked back at Santana with sympathy and compassion. She knew that he would be in the severe pain in the next few days. Simfany was glad that the man who shot Santana was dead because the city would have hell to pay if she had to turn over rocks to find the shooter.

"Ma—ma!" Santana called with all his might.

"My bad, baby boy, I was lost for a minute. What's up, baby? Momma been missing you!" she said as she held his hand and rubbed his head.

"I been missing you too. Right now I guess that morphine helping. But I know I'm going to be sore than a muthafucka later on." He smiled a slight grin and continued.

"But that bandage shit for the birds. I swear that shit hurt like a bitch. I almost bit that nigga." Santana tried to laugh; he grabbed his stomach and grimaced at the pain.

"Fuck that shit." Simfany rubbed around the wound on his abdomen. She knew this wound was the most lethal of the two. Her son was lucky, shit, they both were.

"Let the pain killers work, get some rest. Your body is begging for it. I will be here when you wake up." She rubbed his forehead until he drifted off. Simfany stared into the face of her only angel left in life. She would gladly trade her life for his. She hated the thought, but she knew one day it could be reality. The maternal instinct is always to sacrifice yourself for your offspring.

Simfany was beat from the day's activities. She pulled a chair closer to the hospital bed; she got as comfortable as the chair would allow. Simfany drifted as she rubbed Santana's clammy hands.

***

The night rose and fell quickly as Santana woke up drenched in sweat from a nightmare he was just having. He reached to wipe his mouth from the spittle that came from a deep sleep and found that his hands had IV's attached to them. He began to panic; he attempted to rise but the aching in his stomach was so extreme that he stayed still for the moment. *What the fuck!* he thought to himself. It all began to come back to him now as he breathed and cleared his mind. The scene at the Shop N Go flashed into his brain. He thought it was a dream, a bad dream. But it was now a cold reality that he almost lost life not even twenty-four hours prior. *Damn, you got to be more careful, Tana. You almost died over a nigga you barely knew.* He scorned himself for the stupid actions of his past few days. N.O. was a cool nigga, but he wasn't worth Santana's life. Now all he could think about was whether he would be charged for killing dude over N.O.'s bullshit. He remembered talking to his mother last night, but wasn't sure if the image was real or not. He glanced over and looked toward the chair that sat beside the his hospital bed. It was empty. His mother must have gone and got something to eat or he was just tripping. The morphine bag dripped, and almost instantly, Santana felt his pain ease. He closed his eyes and succumb to the effects of the morphine.

The detective watched from the shadows of the of the second wing near *Room 230*. He watched the reaction of the child as he woke and realized that he was in a hospital bed shot. The fear that permeated his face not only put doubt in his mind about his involvement, but it painted a clear picture of a child than a killer. As he investigated the double homicide that took place the day before, all fingers pointed at a gun battle between the two deceased, wounding the child in the process of the confrontation. But then there was one account saying that the boy killed the young man that started the shooting as he rounded the corner to finish the job. To him the account had to be wrong because Justice Torres was tested for gun powder residue upon entry into the hospital. That's what he was told at least. The only sleep he got that night was in the chairs of the waiting room in CAMC. To any other detective the case would already be solved, but to him he wanted to know more if there was more to know. He didn't believe that the child killed the deceased young man, and truthfully couldn't blame him if he did. What he wanted was the whole story. As he watched Santana close his eyes, he made a mental note to come back and check on the juvenile in a few hours. He needed a statement from him about the incident that occurred. Right now he was a victim and just in case the story got around of him being a killer, he may need protection from revenge of family and friends of the deceased. The detective walked away to the nurse's station.

"When the young man in *Room 230* opens his eyes again, can you please contact me. My name and number is on this card. Thank you." He reached into his blazer and produced a CPD card with his name and contact info on it. The nurse took it and sat it on the counter.

"I will, gladly, officer." She looked at the card again. "Officer Williams," she stated and smiled at him with a beautiful white smile. He smiled back and mouthed a *thank you*. He walked out the hospital into a bright brisk day.

"Damn, another day." Detective Williams sighed and walked to his car with home as his destination. To him it was just another day, but in Charleston and for the families that had to bury their loved ones, that day meant heartache and pain. The saddened violence that plagued America had hit Charleston for the first time that year, claiming the life of not one black soul, but two. The reaper was at work. If only the dead knew they would die before they woke, maybe they would live life to its fullest. The lost souls that would plague the city of 50,000 residents were only to begin. It was going to be a long and hot summer, and the lives of many would be up for grabs.

Chapter Twelve

As Drew walked into Mt. Zion Cemetery in West Baltimore, his eyes teared. He not only lost Kane, but now he also lost the two men that raised them into the gangsters they became. He had only been home two weeks when tragedy struck the Shotgun Crip organization again. This time harder than expected, taking the two most prolific members that they had. The Murphy twins were killed in what looked like an home invasion. The news reported that they were tied up and executed.

Drew stood and stared at the matching head stones of his uncles. The murder rate was at an all time high between the racked up bodies that the county and the city combined. The beginning of the year was proving to be a deadly one. Drew pulled out a bottle of Hennessey and a pre-rolled Dutch Master. He tipped the bottle of liquor up and poured half of liquor on one of the sides and did the same to the other, only leaving a light gulp for himself to ease the pain. He swallowed the brown liquor as he closed his eyes and rubbed his tear stricken face as the liquid warmed his body. The thoughts that invaded Drew's mind were the ugliest kind. He sat down in the grass between the head stones and pulled his knees to his chest. He lit the blunt and deeply inhaled, letting the best of the best do its work. Drew sat there and thought about all the good times he had with his uncles. They were the reason why the whole Washington Park wanted to be Crip. Duke and Donavan Murphy showed unconditional love to all the lives they touched, but they were about that action when the time presented itself. Drew could remember the times when his mother would run Duke out the house for smoking around him. And Donavan—he was a whole another story. Drew's mom use to catch him hiding guns all over the house on some paranoid shit.

Drew laughed at the thought. The memories also killed him deeply. He would miss his mentors. Not only did he lose his right-hand—Kane, but he lost the only two niggaz that really loved him. He wanted revenge and if it took for his casket to drop in the process then so be it. Because he was definitely gone die about this one. Drew inhaled again and closed his eyes. The weed momentarily eased the pain. He closed his eyes and let the weed take him away. He needed to clear his mind because before the night was over, the soul of a Tree Top Piru will separate from his body. Drew had no proof, but he wasn't the police; he didn't need to be convinced by reasonable doubt. Ever since the death of Hood, Piru and Stacks, the gang been running round firing on everybody, leaving bodies in the wake.

Drew wasn't officially Crip yet. But he was raised into the lifestyle of Loccin'. And the twins death not only sealed his initiation, but also sealed his fate as a man. He now fully understood the determination that plagued Santana throughout all those years. Drew couldn't really say for sure, but he knew in his heart that Hood, Piru and Stacks were the product of his little man. He smiled for the first time thinking about his brother from another. Drew rose off his feet and wiped his face. He checked his hip for the Sig Sauer .40 he had planted there and spoke to his uncles' tombstones.

"Look, Cuz, I don't know what happened and how these niggaz got both of y'all. All I can say is I will be sending these niggaz ya way, so be ready for'em. I love y'all nigga, cuz. I was taught every-thing I know by you two men." Drew shook his head side to side. He pulled on his blunt again and laid it in between the two head stones. "Share that shit. I love you, Duke, I love you Don . . . Forever! You hear me, cuz?" Drew nodded as if they could nod back and walked off. It was time to shed blood and make the city cry. *When you embark on a journey of revenge, dig two graves,* Drew thought of Santana's favorite quote. It hailed from the great philosopher Confucius. He understood now more than ever, and he would be ready to die for the cause of his revenge. He stood for his team and no bitch resided in Drew. Now was time to show and tell.

***

Detective Ramos sat at home pondering over the scribbled mes-sages left by his deceased partner. *Damn, Lawson, what the fuck did you get caught up in that got you killed, man?* he thought to himself as he continued to decipher his fallen partner's notes. One thing he seem to get was the web that had each name connected in some way or fashion. The web made more sense than anything else. Byrd was connected to some gang by the name of T.T.P., Jim Dog was also somehow connected to the bunch. But what he couldn't understand was how Simfany was connected to Byrd and the gang. He knew knowledge of Simfany and Jim Dog having issues which brought Santana into the mix, but really nothing more. Ramos began to make notes of his own. The picture was there; he just needed to make it a little more clear. *Where did Simfany live after she got shot?* he asked himself as he searched through the loose paper work. He fingered through more of the file as the hours passed. When he was ready to give up, he stumbled upon a page that had splattered coffee all over it. It was the clue he was looking for; the piece of paper gave the location of where Simfany Vasquez was staying after she was shot. Havre De Grace Maryland. As he read further into the report, he jolted up. What the fuck! He sat straight up and wiped the sleep out of his eyes. He needed to be sure he was reading the report right. The report stated:

Approx. 1 a.m. Surveillance of Carol Washington home . . .
Re: Simfany Vasquez: friend and occupant. Also victim of West Baltimore shooting on Edmondson and Carey.
Subject walks from home to conduct a meeting with known drug King Pin Carlos Rivera?
Known personal driver and henchman present / greets Ms. Vasquez, and pat down for weapons before entry.
Subject in car for 7 to 11 minutes max. Subject exits car and goes back into the home of Carol Washington.
Note: No visual of Carlos R.
Note: The connections of these people are beginning to get extremely deep. Federal help? Tell Ramos?
Shots fired on my vehicle shortly after surveillance of Rivera and Vasquez meeting...

Ramos read and reread the file and notes. It was back to square one. He knew more info than what he did, but was now in a different realm of investigation than before. His partner had embarked on a journey he wasn't obviously ready for.

"How the fuck did Simfany know Byrd, Carlos, Jimdog and TTP? This woman knows all of the shadiest characters Baltimore has ever had to offer. No wonder her time in the city was one of destruction. Damn, Lady, you definitely choose the best of the best." Ramos shook his head as he spoke out loud to himself.

Ramos started from the beginning of the file to make sure that he didn't miss any other connections. The last passage he had just read proved that the boredom had almost got the best of him. It proved that Lawson was on to something of substance. The bullets that connected not two, but three murders scenes on the same day within hours of each other had the police chief down his throat. The death of Lawson brought attention to the case that warranted immediate answers, which he had none of. What Ramos felt in his gut was a detective jitter. He didn't know what the file would mount to, but now finally taking his partner's notes seriously he would dig deeper than before to break these cases. There was a secret and he needed to be a part of it. The lost puzzle to the homicides were in the mind, body and soul of a child. Santana had the only answers, or so he thought. Ramos was used to being dealt a hand that he didn't like, but yet still played them as he saw fit. This wouldn't be no different. Ramos smiled as he happily began to read from the beginning, thanking his partner in death.

***

"Come on, child, get ya butt out of the bathroom. You're always taking forever in there!" Tijuana's mother yelled.

"Okay, ma, dang, you always tripping with ya mean self." Tijuana smiled as she opened the door and walked out of the bathroom with her hands in surrender. Nadia Burks smiled at her beautiful daughter and pushed past her laughing.

"Little girl, you are something else. Wait, I'll talk to you when I'm done using this bathroom." Ms. Burke shut the door. Tijuana shook her head at her mother and walked to Kane's room to iron her uniform for work. Since the death of her younger brother, Kane, Tijuana had decided to stay with her mother for comfort and support. What she asked herself all the time was why her mother still lived in Washington Park. When she came up with no plausible reasons, she just let it go and enjoyed her time with her mom. The time was well needed, they needed each other more than anything. As Tijuana pulled the ironing board out of Kane's closet, her mother popped her head into the door way.

"Good morning, beauty, what time do you have to be at work?" Ms. Burke asked as she looked down at Tijuana's stomach.

"At nine o'clock."

"Soooo, did you go to the OBGYN?"

"Yes, I did, mother, and like we thought, I am pregnant. Don't be looking at me like that. I know who the father is, ma'am!" Tijuana said confidently. But in truth she didn't. Around the time she slept with Santana she was involved with Green. In all reality, her and Green was going steady for the most part; what happened with Santana just happened. It wasn't planned or expected. So at this moment it was an up-in-the-air situation. The only thing she was sure about was that she would be keeping her child no matter what. Tijuana hadn't spoken to Simfany or Santana since her surprise visit with him. Tijuana was so lost in her thoughts she didn't hear nothing her mother said.

"Tijuana . . . Ti . . . Juana . . . !" Ms. Burke snapped her fingers in front of her daughter's face, knocking Tijuana out of her momentary state of oblivion.

"My bad, momma, what were you saying?" Tijuana asked sheepishly.

"I said, so what are you planning to do? Have you told the father yet? Like, what's up?" Momma Burke put her hand on her hip and twisted her neck as she waited on a response.

"Why? Of course, I will be keeping my child, and yes, I have told my man about the baby. And gladly he is just as hyped as us. Any more question, Queen Nadia?" Tijuana laughed, trying to disguise her tell-tale face of lies. The truth was, she was scared to approach both Santana and Green. She knew she would have to approach Santana with facts because the kind of respect he demanded was powerful. Green was more a go-with-the-flow kind of man. So she knew if she came at Santana with her pregnancy, she needed to come correct. Which she planned on doing. Tijuana prayed the baby that she was carrying was that of Santana Vasquez. The aura that he put off and his swag was of pure confidence. The loyalty he possessed was only read about in novels. He was a different kind of person, that was for sure. He was the kind of nigga that she dreamed of. He possessed the qualities of a king at such a young age. Tijuana would always tell him that he was a descendant of a past life; he was too level-headed and unique. His mind was advanced to be the tender age of sixteen. She shook from the chills that ran through her body, the thought of him alone drove her crazy. She shook the electricity through her body and finished her task at hand. She didn't want to be late to work. The wonder of a life with Santana made her pussy throb. Tijuana shook out of daze.

"Ma." Tijuana walked around the house looking for her mother. She walked into the living room and saw her mother cleaning .

"Ma, how you just gone leave me in!"

"Girl, listen, you always lost in your thoughts. I let you dream for a minute. Plus you answered the question I wanted to know. As long as you're happy I'm happy. Congratulations, baby, I'm very much excited as you are. I love you, baby."

"Awww, mommy. I love you too. Thank you for the love and encouragement. I got this iron on, let me get ready before I'm late." Tijuana leaned down and hugged the only person she truly loved and had left in this world. Ms. Burke smiled and kissed her only living child on the cheek. Tijuana went into the room and got ready to go to work. The thought of having Santana's baby was exciting and stressful all in the same sense. His future was undecided and very unpredictable. Regardless, like she told him before, she was going to ride until the wheels fell off. And she knew that not having contact with him was going against what she promised him. She made a mental note to call Simfany so she could get in contact with Santana.

The element of death lurked around the corners in the Washington Park complex. The war not only left Crip after Crip fighting for their life, but blood after blood fighting for theirsalso. Each day Tijuana pulled into "The Park", she knew that it could be her last, bullets had no name, and them bitches was flying daily. The body count was so real on this side of town there was a spray-painted wall that sat at the beginning of the train station in Aberdeen. It stated:

"Cross this bridge if you want, but may your soul *Rest In Peace*—Don't get caught lacking."

The message was beyond real. The truth behind it sent chills up every person that crossed the bridge to pass over. Each person knew that all was fair in the love or war. But as the writing on the wall said: *May Your Soul Rest In Peace.*

Jamel Mitchell

Chapter Thirteen

Detective Williams questioned the East End residents, trying to find answers of why the double homicide took place, who the players were and if they missed anything of importance. Detective Williams drove around making his presence known. He knew the neighborhood would talk about him riding through asking questions. That's what he wanted. If it was something to be said, it would be said. And it would get back to him. A lot of people stuck to the code of not talking to the police, but one thing he found as the weakness of every neighbor he ever policed, they all tell someone something.

Williams pulled up to the residence of Cameron Dukes, also known as N.O. He reached into the glove compartment to retrieve the autopsy of N.O. He had received the pictures earlier that day. It was obvious that N.O. was up to no good; he was dressed as a bum. He just needed the angle of why. His superior wanted to close the case altogether because both suspects ended up dead. Williams agreed, but still wanted to make sure that no other parties were involved.

"Why the fuck were you dressed as a bum for, Dukes?" he asked out loud as he looked through the crime scene photos. He shrugged and put the photos and autopsy away. There was something more sinister behind the double homicide that he knew for sure. Whether he could show and prove would be a different story.

As a juvenile, he himself had been in and out of placement homes. His mischievous ways kept him deep in the eyes of the law. At the age of eighteen he decided to take another path. Being away from his family crushed him more than ever. So when he changed and joined the police academy, he was shunned. His family played as if they loved him unconditionally, but really hated the decision that he made. He understood because of the life they still lived. He packed up and left, living and growing on his own. Now twenty years later he was standing in the home of what appears to be a disturbed man. Or so he thought.

Williams walked up the stairs and stood on the porch. The air was brisk, but extremely fresh. He breathed in a deep breath and exhaled slowly. He looked around the small alley, and to his surprise no one

135

paid him any mind. He pulled the key to the town home out his pocket and opened the door. *Damn*, he thought to himself. The house was plush and put together well. The living room alone let him know that the killing was deeper than rap. Detective walked up the stairs where two bedrooms and a bathroom stood. Detective Williams went into the room closest to him. Against the wall sat a 96' entertainment system, and a king size bed near the window. He looked around the room; he lifted the mattress, looked into the closet and drawers. He found nothing of substance. He did the same for the bathroom and the other room. The only thing that he could conclude from the search of the rooms was that the deceased was into a lot and he was paranoid. The other room had monitors and survey cameras that looked into the street in front of his home and the back near the alley way.

Detective Williams was more intrigued than anything. He searched the bottom level as well and came up with nothing. This was some bullshit, he thought, as he exited the home. He walked to his car and placed a call to the hospital; he needed to talk to the juvenile. He needed to shed light on this homicide before he felt at ease to close the case.

Detective Williams pulled off more defeated than before in his life. Something in his heart told him that he was really making a mistake if he closed the case out. On paper it was cut and dry. It was a shoot-out that killed both suspects. Nothing more, nothing less. There is only one other way to go about it and he laid in a hospital with holes in him. He needed Santana to talk. Detective Williams walked back into the hospital only hours after he left. The nurse at the desk called to relay that Santana was up and alert. The entrance to the hospital was one he hated. He hated hospitals altogether. It was a place of pain, agony and death. But it was a place that many lives were saved. The hospital was spacious and neat. While he waited on the elevator, he sent his partner Daniel Schnooer a text message: *Questioning Witness at CAMC. Call when I'm done.* The elevator opened. When Williams looked up, he saw one of the most beautiful of creatures standing in the elevator.

"Good evening, beauty." He was smitten by her beauty.

"Good evening, officer. Here to protect and serve?" She giggled to herself.

"In hopes. Haven't I met you before?" The woman looked very familiar.

"I don't think so, because you have a face that a woman like me couldn't ever forget. Let me stop. What is ya name? You look familiar yourself." The woman batted her eyes and bit her bottom lip.

"My name is Brian Williams. Nice to meet you . . ."

"Katherine, but everyone calls me Kat." Kat extended her hand; he politely took hold and kissed it.

"A pleasure," Detective Williams stated as the elevator opened for his departure.

"Likewise," Kat replied as she followed him off the elevator. The look on his face was priceless. She laughed.

"What!"

She laughed "This is my floor too, cutie."

"Oh, okay, I thought you were stalking me," he joked back.

The two joked all the way to the receptionist desk. Kat handed the detective her phone so that he could put his contact info inside of it. He leaned on the reception desk.

"Good evening, ma'am, I would like to know what room Santana Vasquez—I mean Justice Torres—is being treated in," Kat said. The receptionist looked through the computer.

"He is being held in room 230. Make a right around this desk and go straight to the back and it's the room on the left. Before you go please sign in right here on this line." She handed Kat a clip board. She signed it. She then looked at the detective and mouthed: *Call me*, holding her hand as if it were a receiver. *Oh, believe me, I will* he thought as he watched her walk way.

"Sir, may I help you?" the receptionist from earlier looked up into his eyes with disappointment etched all over them.

"Yes, I'm here to question a victim by the name of Justice Torres." He showed his credentials again. He knew that she had re-membered him by the hatred that he saw in her eyes about Kat.

"Please sign here. He has visitors in there right now if that's not a problem."

"None at all. He is still in *Room 230*, correct?"

"Yes, sir," she said in her most polite voice possible.

"Thank you." He walked to the room by memory. When he got to the door, he looked in confusion. The woman he was talking to was hugged up on his victim. Santana—He could have heard wrong, but he was sure that she said something about a person by the name of Santana. He turned around and walked back to the receptionist desk.

"May I help you, officer?" she asked with an attitude.

"The female that talked to you asked for what patient you have here?" The receptionist looked at the clip board.

"She went to visit Mr. Justice Torres."

"No, what I meant to ask is, what name did she ask about first." The receptionist typed until she was able to pull up the name that was in the search memory.

"She asked about a patient by the name of Sant—hold on may I ask why you are asking this question."

"I'm investigating a homicide that may or may not—" He was out off .

"No disrespect, Mr.—"

"Williams."

"Mr. Williams—but I'm not allowed to disclose any of that kind of information. I was under the presumption that you were together in some way, shape or form. I apologize sincerely for the confusion. As I said before, she signed in to see a patient by the name of Justice Torres. With that said are you going to question your victim or will you like to come back after his visitors are gone?"

"No, ma'am, I will be going back there right now to ask my questions. Thank you very much for your help and I apologize also for the third degree. It was nothing, honestly."

"Umm huh. You're welcome." Detective Williams walked back to *Room 230*; he watched for a second as they interacted. When he didn't see anything of suspicion, he knocked on the door. The people in the room looked up. When Kat's eyes caught his, she looked on in confusion.

"Good evening, my name is Detective Williams, I have a few question for Mr. Torres about the double homicide that took place a couple of days ago. May I?"

"Yes, please come in." Simfany got out of her seat and offered it to him.

"No, thank you, ma'am, I don't plan on being here that long. I just have a few questions to ask Justice."

"Should he be worried about anything?"

"Such as what, ma'am?" he asked inquisitively.

"Like retaliation because he was there when the shooting happened. Or anything of that sort?" Simfany played the concerned mom.

"I pray not, ma'am, as I know both of the assailants were pronounced dead. I'm just here to connect a few dots, ma'am."

"Yes, sir."

"How are you feeling? I want to say sorry on behalf of the Charleston Police Department that you were dragged into this situation. But I do have some questions that need to be answered. They may be frivolous to you but it can mean a lot to me. So please answer truthfully. You okay with that?" He looked Santana in his eyes as he laid in the bed hurting. Santana looked at his mother. She nodded her approval.

"Okay, what do you wanna know?"

"To your best ability can you tell me what happened?"

"So I walked to Gino's to order some food. During the wait I went across the street to buy me some Iced Tea and candy for a friend. I also bought a beer for—"

"I'm not worried about that. Continue please, this can very much help me."

"Okay, I bought the bum dude a beer because I didn't want to just give him money. When I walked out the store I saw this dude looking shady as hell standing at the pay phone, but I paid him no mind because at this point I'm used to the strange looks. Being from New York I get a few asshole looks. I didn't think nothing of it. I put my plastic bag on the ground to give the bum the beer I bought for him, and felt my stomach explode followed by the blast. After I fell, the bum grabbed me to the ground and shielded my body. I heard a few more gun shots and felt my face get wet. After the shooting stopped, I got up to run but collapsed. I don't know how I got to the hospital, but I am very thankful I made it."

"So you didn't recognize any one else around that wasn't shot that looked suspicious?"

"No, sir. I was at the wrong place at the wrong time."

"Okay, I was also told by a few eye witnesses that you possessed a gun that day in question. Did you fire your gun?" Detective Williams asked aggressively.

"I've never owned or shot a gun in my life, sir. So whoever claimed that is either lying or fabricating the truth," Santana said innocently.

"Sir, do I need to retain a lawyer for my son? He was shot and almost killed in cold blood and you're here to interrogate him? What kind of policing is this!" Simfany exclaimed. She was furious by his line of questioning.

"Ma'am, I'm not here to accuse. I was simply asking if the account was a true one. I do have a job to do, ma'am. I have to make sure that when your son gets out this hospital bed that he is safe. If I heard that rumor, then anyone could have heard it. The streets talk. I know that your son didn't fire a gun that day but I don't know if he was in possession of one. I'm sorry if the questions are difficult or even out of pocket, but they have to be asked." Williams tried to relay his intentions as easily as possible without overstepping his boundaries. He had to remember it was a sixteen-year-old child laid in that hospital bed.

"Please finish your questioning. My son will need his rest." Without missing a beat he continued.

"Did you know Cameron Dukes in any way?"

"Who? I don't know who that is."

"It was the man dressed as a bum."

Simfany interjected. "What do you mean a man that was dressed up as a bum? So he wasn't really a bum?" She acted as if she was confused.

"Yes, ma'am the two men that killed each other was into a feud from many years ago. Cameron Dukes was dressed up in bum attire, as I have investigated. He was like that for many months since being released from prison." By the looks on the faces of those present, he knew that no more questions needed to be asked. They were all baffled or seemed to be.

"Oh, this shit is deep. Now I understand the line of questioning." Sirnfany acted as if she now understood what was going on. Santana laughed at his mother in her *Academy Award* performance. Santana's body hurt instantly from the laugh.

"Awww, fuck." Santana grimaced.

"If I have any more questions can I come back and see you?" Detective Williams had no reason to be there any longer. He realized that Justice was a victim and just a kid. He would follow a few more hunches but would declare the case closed.

"Yes, sir, if you ever need anything answered I will be at 1536 Jackson," Kat answered slyly. He laughed at her forwardness.

"Thank you, every one, for your cooperation. Again I hope you get well soon, son!" Detective Williams said with sympathy.

"Thank you also, officer," Raven added from the back of the pack.

Detective Williams left the hospital room. When he cleared the door way he stopped on the side to text his partner a summary of what took place. Then, as if on cue, Raven spoke.

"Is it me or did he come in here trying to accuse Santana of murder. Because that shit he was on sounded like some bullshit." Raven was vexed. He listened intently.

"No, he was just here doing his job, sweetheart. There is nothing for Santana to hide. He was a victim in some shit these country ass niggaz got going on. Wrong place, wrong time." Simfany assured her. "Don't worry, beauty, he's not in any trouble. This time his bad ass didn't do anything. Especially not murder. It's okay, love."

"But ain't that nigga fine as hell?" Kat interjected. They all burst out laughing. He even smiled at the comment. He knew he would have fun with her. She was very eccentric.

"For real though that nigga look like Idris Elba. Don't he?" Kat asked.

"Kat, you sound thirsty as hell. You too sexy to sound like that, boo. He is okay though. Don't be trying throw pussy on that nigga,

you know how you get." Simfany and Raven laughed uncontrollably. Santana tried but couldn't. Detective Williams had heard
enough. He finished his summary and walked off. He would be closing the case once and for all. There was no reason for him to feel as
Santana had anything to do with the double homicide. There was a
GSR took upon entry, which indicated none was found. That alone
would eliminate a suspect, but he still wanted to be more than certain. Detective Williams walked out the hospital satisfied with the
outcome of his day.

***

Devon Sanders paced the floor in the basement of the abandoned
house. He was furious. His little brother had been killed on a mission.
Devon wanted to pay a nigga to slay N.O. but his little brother Breeze
wanted the confirm kill on his own hands. N.O. had killed their big
cousin when they were only kids. The plan that they orchestrated obviously went wrong. Now he paced quietly as his men watched in
silence. No one had any explanation to the death of Breeze. What
fucked him up more than anything was, the little nigga didn't go on
the drill by himself. He was accompanied by another one of his
friends. Fatty Man was a known shooter born and raised on Charleston's East End. The confusion was eating at him. He had to get his
shit together before he summoned his men. He didn't want to act out
of emotion. He took pride in being a boss. So he took a few days to
handle his family, his emotions and the arrangements for his brother's
burial.

"So now we sit all looking sad and stupid over yet another body
that has dropped in our team. This one being very close to my heart.
I need answers, my nigga. What have niggaz heard?" Von asked sin-
isterly. "Come on, my nigga, not every fucking body speak at once!"
Von exclaimed. One of his soldiers stepped up.

"The little bitch I fuck with said that this Fat ass nigga let Breeze
get dribbled by the little nigga that survived." He stepped back in line.
Von's face turned sour. He looked over the crowd. Fatty Man was
already on his shit list because Breeze got killed in his care. Now to

hear that Fatty could have somehow saved or got retribution for Breeze infuriated him. Fatty Man looked at Remy with the illest intent. At that moment Fatty promised himself that if he made it out the bando he would end Remy's career. It was if Remy read his mind; he smiled at the thought. He knew what he was about to relay would for sure get Fatty killed. Von picked up on the tension between his two soldiers.

"Fuck you mugging that nigga for? He spoke on what he heard, it's what the streets you love saying about you, cuz. You're my little brother's right-hand man. You was supposed to protect that nigga or die with him. What the flick happened, bruh?" Fatty just sat there looking stupid.

"Nigga, I said what the fuck happened out there?" Von yelled and pulled his gun, training on Fatty's face.

"Whoa, bruh. This me, my nigga. I don't know what Nessy heard, but my brother got killed that day too, Von. I would have never let bruh end like that without sliding to the best of my ability. If anybody know better, you k–" his words got drowned out by the phone that blared in Remy's pocket. The look that appeared on Remy's face was one of pure terror. He knew phones were to be turned off completely, especially during a meeting.

"You gone answer the phone since you just don't fucking listen!" Remy pulled his phone out his pocket to power it off until he saw that Nessy was the caller.

"Cuz, it's Nessy calling. I was supposed to give her this cheese and trees to take to Lil' Manny at he jail. The meeting was called on a short notice." Remy explained nervously. He wasn't trying to catch no DP's, especially not during this time of grief.

"Perfect. Answer and have her tell you what she heard again. I wanna hear it from her mouth." Von steadily held the gun on Fatty. Remy answered and put it on speaker.

"What's up, Ness?"

"Nigga, don't *what's up-Ness* me. Where the fuck you at? I'm suppose to go see Manny in a few hours. Take that dick outta whatever bitch you with and meet me!" Ness said venomously.

"Chill, cuz, you trippin' ."

"I ain't ya damn cuz, nigga!" Nessy yelled back.

"Cuz, you trippin', I'm on the East trying to find out if what you told me was valid about the day Breeze got killed." Remy locked eyes with Von.

"I told you what happened already. I was right there. What? You don't believe me or something?" You could hear the annoyance in Nessy's voice.

"Nah, bae, I'm not saying that. To be honest I was drowning in liquor that night. I wanted to ask the East what the word was again. I didn't feel like getting cussed out by you because you thought a nigga wasn't listening. Fuck it, to end this shit tell me what you saw, not heard. Talking all that you was there shit." Remy held the phone out for everyone in the room to hear clearly. He knew what she was about to say; he just wanted to make sure everyone else would hear the same shit.

"Okay, remember I told you I had to go the store for—"

"Nessy. Why you was there is not important. I wanna know what you seen, Shorty."

"Rude ass nigga. Whatever. I was going to the store across the street when I seen Breeze and Fatty looking suspicious as hell. Breeze acted like he was on the pay phone while Fatty Man looked up and down the street looking hot with his fat ass. Anyway the little sexy light-skinned OT nigga came out of Shop-N-Go with a beer and some other shit in a bag. He walked over to where a bum or what seemed to be a bum was laid at. He bent over to hand him something and-Breeze pulled his strap and shot the little nigga in his back. The bum pulled dude to the ground and shot back. Breeze banged a few more shots. I don't know if he hit anything else because I took cover for a second. That's when I saw Breeze run behind Shop-N-Go and Fatty ran up Ruffner. I seen Breeze come out the alley on the side and shoot the bum in the head. He paused for a second with his gun aimed at the little nigga. I don't know what happened or if anything was said, but I saw the little nigga raise a gun and hit Breeze in his chest and face. As he got shot, he let off another shot that connected with dude. I'm sorry that happened to Breeze, Remy." She sniffled back tears.

Remy put his feelings aside and continued his questioning.

"What happened after that?"

"I tried to call you first, but when you didn't answer, I followed him. He stumbled up the street. I seen him run to that Saint's whip the one nigga be in. Fuck—what's his name again?" It took her a second, so Remy helped her.

"You talking bout N.O.?"

"Yeah, that's him. When he got in the car, he just sat there. I tried to call you a few more times, but of course you were probably with one of those bitches of yours." Nessy sighed deeply. She also had seen Zach come drive him to the hospital, but she would leave that part out. She didn't know what would happened to the OT nigga, but if what she figured would happen, then she didn't want Zach caught up in the fire.

"Did the nigga Fatty bang at all?" Remy looked at Fatty, knowing the question would seal his fate. He didn't give a fuck regardless. He was tired of Fatty running around the city like he was a killer, but Remy knew he was a bitch for real. He deserved a coward's death.

"No, I didn't see him shoot. It was a lot of shots though so I don't—"

"That's all I needed. I'll bang at you in a minute. Give me about an hour—"

"Whatever. Don't fucking cut me off!" she stated angrily and hung up. Remy turned his phone off and step back into the line. Von's eyes misted. Breeze was his blood brother, but damn Fatty Man was also like his brother. The decision was hard to make. He wanted him dead for his coward ass actions. He wanted to hear Fatty's truth.

"What you have to say about that, nigga?" Von asked with a face full of tears.

"Bruh, it didn't go down like that. Lil' Breeze started to shoot, I saw the mist from the bodies on the ground. The nigga N.O. didn't send no shots back, cuz. Nessy lied about that. When Breeze rounded the corner to the alley, I thought the mission was complete. He ran one way and I ran the other like we rehearsed. We was already out there looking dumb as shit. It was still light outside, Von. Fuck was I suppose to do? He wasn't shot while I was there. I thought he ran—"

Fatty put his head down and started to cry. The loss of Breeze hit him more than anyone in the basement. He loved that nigga since they went to Piedmont Elementary together. They took care of him when his mother abandoned him.

Von knew how close they all were, that's why it hurt him so much that he heard that Fatty abandoned Breeze. He lowered the gun and began to walk out the room, but then stopped and looked back at a surprised Fatty.

"Nigga, I can't sit here and act like this shit don't hurt. I didn't only lose one brother that day; I lost two. I was always taught to crush any and everyone that ain't family. This ya one pass. You have till tonight to get ya shit together and get the fuck out this state. If anyone sees you around here, you will be killed. I hate this for you. I know you and Remy got some whack ass jealous shit going on, so I know to take what I heard with a grain of salt. One thing for sure, you left bruh to die alone. You can't live here no longer." He turned and walked up the stairs and out of the basement. Fatty turned and looked at Remy. He didn't see no fear in Remy, but the look alone let niggaz know what it was. Fatty Man laughed to himself.

"You already know what time it is when I catch you, cuz," Fatty said as he followed Von out the basement.

"I"ll be ready for ya bitch ass. You the one that let cuz get dribbled, you bitch ass nigga!" Remy yelled after Fatty. Remy already knew that he would have to be on point. Fatty was a killer by all means of the word. What happened that day was up in the air. It was the word of Nessy, the most prolific hood rat the hood ever seen. She lied and stole to get the shit she wanted on more than one occasion. One thing she did was keep it a band with the homies, though. They had all flicked her at one point. Whether her account was authentic or fabricated, no one would ever know. The decision was made. What Von said was law. If anyone saw Fatty after the day was over, his order was to kill on sight. Childhood friend or not, he meant every word spoken.

Chapter Fourteen

A few weeks out the hospital, Santana began his healing process. He so badly needed to rehab his shocked limbs into cooperating with him. Though he wasn't fully healed, he was on a strong path of recovery. The thought of almost dying made him look into a broader day, but the demon in him made him even more callous at heart. His emotions were all over the place. The experience humbled him, also putting him on the side of reality. The lives he took gave him the sense of being untouchable. Being shot and staring in the eyes of the grim reaper was one thing altogether; being on the opposite side of the gun made him look at shit differently wholeheartedly. Santana being shot convinced Simfany to rent a home close by, not exactly in the city limits but close enough to nurse her son back to health. Simfany tried time after time to get Santana to leave West Virginia, but he refused. The attempts fell on deaf ears. Detective Williams closed the case in the deaths of N.O. and Breeze, so Santana saw no reason in fleeing
yet again. Plus he didn't want to have to reestablish himself again somewhere else. He was cool in his situation, bullets and all.

Santana, Zach and Haseem clicked on all cylinders. Haseem and Zach did their best to restore Santana's sanity back to its original state. He was a handful; that was for sure. The love and trust that grew between the three men was one Simfany couldn't even falter. But with the bond came jealousy and envy. The city watched and the niggaz that grew up under Haseem and Zach began to feel a certain kind of way. Though Santana was hurt, he still helped put food on his brethren's table. The trio linking would cause the demise and down fall of many, leaving a history forged in blood.

***

"What's good, son? What's on the menu for tonight?" Santana asked from the passenger seat of Zach's 2001 Ford Explorer.

"Man, this pretty boy ass nigga always trying hit somebody bitch. You need to stop playing and wife Darla badass up. She always at ya house anyway." Haseem laughed. "As matter of a fact, bruh, both of you pretty boy ass niggaz better sit away from mine!" Haseem said with slight humor in his voice, but they knew his tender dick ass was serious.

"Bruh, if you don't shut ya lil' skinny, big, mothball breath smelling, Rumpelstiltskin head having . . ." they all burst out laughing before Zach could finish his joke.

"Fuck both you niggaz, bruh, for real. But on a more serious note I was at my uncle Charlie's house and man, I seen the most money I had ever seen in my life there today. Some nigga named Torrey was there. An ol' fat mufucka too. They counted like a hundred thousand when I was there, or so I thought it was. I'm probably overexaggerating that shit, but I know it was different kind of money than we're used to. Bruh, tell me y'all for the caper? Tana, I know you rocking with me, right?" Haseem scooted up, looking at Santana from the back seat. He knew if anyone was down it would be Santana. As of recent events, Santana tried to fall back and stay out the way. He was still wanted for multiple murders in another state. He had got lucky after he got shot that he wasn't picked up and shipped. So he proceeded with caution and thought about his actions for the first time since a young child.

"Nigga, the real question is, is you rocking when them same niggas try and come get that hundred bands back? Because you might be down to ride against local dudes, but what about niggas you can't see coming?" Santana let that marinate. "Because let me tell you something I've learned, you country ass niggas are slick. Zach, tell Heem how I even met N.O. as a bum, my nigga laying in front of Shop-N-Go. I would have never seen him coming and you wouldn't believe how I play in these streets. I just look like this." Santana laughed hysterically. Zach laughed with him because he thought he'd seen a glimpse, but in all reality neither men knew what type killer he really was. It had tickled him internally.

"Heem, that nigga right, bruh. You gotta be prepared for a war after that. You ready for that because I ain't to be honest. Y'all my niggaz, so I will always keep it a hundred with you. I ain't built for no war. You been my nigga since hide and seek, bruh, so I'll ride with you regardless. Just don't get me killed!" Zach explained as he whipped through the West Side hill. The three sat in silence as everyone processed what Zach had just said. The truth was, Zach wasn't trying to be a part of no shit that could get him killed. He knew if a nigga had that kind of money, he was an easy check. Santana wasn't down for the robbery neither, but he knew that if they did decide to go, he would be there. He didn't want them to get their lives taken because they were built different. He was loyal by default in this situation. Santana told himself that he would speak nothing further on the matter. If they went, he went. Santana had other shit on his head than the talk of robbing a nigga. For the first time in years he and his mother had got into a bad argument earlier that day.

Twelve Hours Earlier—

"What you call yourself doing, Santana?" Simfany asked angrily in her navy blue and pink Couture shorts. Simfany had just come back from Maryland from visiting Tijuana and her mother. The news that she had for Santana was a constant on her mind, that was until she actually seen him.

"What are you talking about?" he slurred his words walking out of his room. Simfany was vexed to say the least.

"First of, you bitch ass nigga, you wobbling around this muthafucka high, after a nigga dead or alive shed blood from ya skin. You don't know what the streets seen, said or relayed. Secondly, you just out right slipping, baby boy. Let me explain something to you, nigga, you area-fucking-out-of-towner! Do you hear me? This isn't ya city. Stop acting as though you're comfortable out here before I make ya dumb ass relocate. I refuse to lose my son because you wanna run around here smelling ya nuts. "

"Let me tell you something, mother! I'm fucking grown. I live how I want. I go and please as I want. If I wanna get high as you . . . you call it—I 'm not going—" Santana's words slurred more as he staggered around the living room trying to find a seat. Simfany just looked
on. Santana was breaking her heart. He was becoming too reckless.

Her motherly intuition was giving her bad vibes.

"Santana, look at you. I didn 't raise you to be like this. Drugs ain't what we do, baby boy." Simfany finally went over to help her son find a resting place. "I just want you to grasp the reality of what is going on. Because you are losing touch. Do you hear me? You losing touch." She looked into her son's eyes. It hurt bad to see that Santana was following the path of so many others.

"I love you, baby." Simfany held Santana while she rocked back and forth. Santana shrugged out her embrace.

"Leave me alone. You slipping. Stop talking to me like that. I know what I got going on." Santana tried to stand and feel.

"What the fuck are you high on anyway?" Simfany asked suspiciously. It didn't look like he was drunk like she first thought.

"I was drinking," he replied. Simfany leaned in further to smell him. There was no alcohol evident. He was lying.

"Oh, so now we lying to each other?" Simfany pulled away from him. She looked him over for a second, then grabbed his chin and looked him in the eyes.

"Nigga, what the fuck you high on?" Santana finally got to his fieet. She asked again.

"Nigga, what the fuck are you high on?" When he didn't answer, she shoved him down into the love seat face first.

"You don't wanna answer me, huh?" she tapped his pocket one by one. When she hit his back pocket, it rattled. She felt instant disappointment. Simfany knew the sound all too well. She went into his pocket and pulled the pill bottle out. Simfany glared at her son.

"Nigga, you got me fucked up. How could you—" she choked back her cry. She was hurt. She got over the initial shock and opened the bottle. The bottle contained small blue Xanax pills. The bottle was half full, which meant to her that he'd been using them for a while. Simfany could do nothing but laugh at the shit. This nigga had lost his damn mind. It was comical that she had to admit. Nothing needed to be said. She sat the pill bottle on the counter, then walked to him in his haze. She pulled his gun off his hip and also put it on the counter next to the pills. It made her mad that he was getting complacent with all that was going on. Simfany couldn't be as vexed if he had more control of the situation; she would still be pissed, regardless, *but damn he was slipping to the highest degree.* He laid on the couch helpless. Simfany looked at her son once more and shook her head in disgust. Simfany cried. She was happy that she was about to be a grandmother; she just hoped Santana got his shit together so he could be a father.

Santana sat oblivious to the way his mother felt. He enjoyed his high. The slamming of the front door had little effect on his current state. He didn't care. *I'm grown, fuck what she talking 'bout* was all he could think as he drifted into a somber sleep. He knew he was out of pocket. But at that moment of bliss he didn't quite care.

Santana sat in the car with Haseem and Zach trying to forget his earlier episode, not only with his mother but the lag of the pills. The way the pills took him off-guard and out of character, his mother was right, they weren't meant for him. All he could think about was when Simfany disarmed him. In his mind he wanted to stop her, but couldn't. His body didn't react. He was too high to defend himself. Lesson learned, that's for sure. His pill popping days were over.

Santana pulled his phone out his pocket and tried to call his mother. She sent him to voicemail. She hadn't talked to him since. She was mad and he knew that. He also understood.

"Aye, bruh . . . Tana . . . Bruh." Haseem hit his shoulder. Santana looked up.

"What's good, son?"

"Bruh, I'm Uncle Charlie nephew. They'll let me in. This shit will be the easiest lick we could ever hit. The spot right around the corner. You down?" Haseem asked excitedly.

"Son, you still talking 'bout that damn lick?"

"Bruhhhh, that's what I said," Zach seconded.

"My nigga, I know you good and you've looked out, but I want my own money. Plus I just see this shit for what it is. easy cheese. Either y'all in or I'm gone do it by myself," Haseem said in a matter-of-fact tone.

"I definitely won't let you slide in there by your lone self. Can't do that. I got you, I'm there!" Santana replied. Zach sighed. He was pissed. He didn't want to go into no one's trap spot and take shit.

"Fuck it, bruh. I'm there!" Zach said, shaking his head. He knew the idea was a bad one. Zach glared at Haseem in the back seat. Haseem looked up. He was wrong and he knew it. He was playing off of the information he told him about Santana. Zach had told Haseem of the events that led up to N.O's death and Santana's shooting. Haseem knew that Santana would most likely be down for the caper. Zach shook his head and pulled into the complex.

Santana sat in the passenger seat looking out the window. He thought about the "lick" that they were about to go on. The words *stay out of trouble* just didn't register to him. It seemed like that was the last thing he did. He was barely done healing from the shells that he had lodged inside of him. Santana just loved the thought of playing with fire. There was no reason that he should be riding shotgun to go rob any one. His mother had money, and he knew all he had to do was call. Whatever he wanted could be tangible as long as it was in the realm of reason.

"So what kind of shit we 'bout to get ourselves into?" Santana asked, wanting to know the probability of him having to use his gun. And if he did, to what extent were they ready to go?

"Shit, bruh, this shit 'bout to be a cake walk. My uncle Charlie be at this spot. He know everyone in there, so they gone let me in. But I would still be ready for whatever though, if that's what you're asking." Haseem answered nonchalantly. *This lil' nigga acting like he a wild wild west type nigga. We gone see.* Santana laughed at his thought. He'd seen through the bullshit. The smile was a fake one. He was fucked up inside. The conversation he had with his mother continued to weigh on his heart. He didn't like to argue with his raise about nothing. He knew for sure he was lacking and he would definitely take heed to her worries.

The car came to a stop, breaking Santana out of his thoughts and back on the task at hand. Out of habit he reached into his waist and grabbed his gun; it wasn't the Glock he was used to. He had left that at the scene on N.O.'s person. Nonetheless, though, he was prepared. He checked the clip and it indicated that he had at least eight to give back at the sight of danger. No one knew Santana and what he was really capable of, even after the Shop-N-Go situation. The city just felt like he got shot, just a victim in the middle of someone else's business. An innocent bystander, as you may call it. He laughed often about the misconstrued notion. Santana also knew that he was lucky that Breeze hesitated. In truth he should be sitting in someone's grave somewhere or awaiting the trial of his life.

They all got out of the car and walked to the home in question. It was a small complex of some sort. The homes were made in a horse shoe kind of setting with the Kanawha River sitting on its backside. Santana looked at the river; it was pure black. The coolness that came off of it made Santana shiver slightly. Santana and Zach took their positions on the side of the door as Haseem knocked. The door was answered almost immediately.

"Who is it?" a male's voice asked from the other side.

"It's Charlie's nephew unk." Haseem instantly recognized the voice. He knew that he would gain access without trouble. He heard the locks being unbolted. When the door opened, the man stood there; he moved aside for Haseem to enter. Santana didn't know what he was supposed to do next, so he did the only thing that came to mind. He pulled his gun and put it to the man's face. Zach put his finger to his lips, advising him to keep quite. Santana moved forward pushing the man into the home, gun pressed to his head.

"Turn around." The man did as he was told. The fear on his face said it all.

"Nigga, you bet not, I will push ya shit back. You hear me?" Santana said in a hushed tone. The man nodded in agreement.

"Unk, who was that at the door?" another man called from a room adjacent to the living room. Haseem pointed to the door to the left and put his finger to his mouth, telling Zach and Santana to remain quiet.

"It's me, Cmore, uncle Charlie's nephew!" Haseem called from the living room.

"Oh, okay, when they let ya badass out the detention center?" Cmore said happily. The men heard him walking to open the door. They braced for bullshit. What Cmore saw broke his heart more than anything. He looked at Haseem with daggers. He shook his head. The disappointed look said enough, no words needed to be spoken. Cmore took off back into the room. Santana left the old head and sprinted for the door before it closed. He caught the door and trained the gun on Cmore.

"Old head, chill, we not trying hurt you, blood. But know if you make me, I will. So please sit ya ass down on that bed." The look in Santana's eyes said it all. He was not playing whatsoever. Cmore sat down, but never taking his eyes off of Santana or the gun he held.

"Shorty, don't be on no hero shit over some shit that ain't even yours. Tell us what we want to know and we will be gone out as fast as we came." Santana tried his best to reassure him.

"What y'all want?" Cmore asked, sitting bolt upright in his bed. You could tell the man was restless from the day's earlier events.

"Son, you know why we here. Stop playing fucking dmnb. That's the shit that's gone get you hurt!" Santana said menacingly. Santana calmed himself down; he wasn't trying to catch no more bodies. His soul held enough bullshit. He heard Zach and Haseem ravaging through the house. He laughed to himself; they were breaking shit and all.

"Yo, son, come watch this nigga while I look around!" Santana yelled as he eyed Cmore. He was itching in all reality to squeeze his gun. He wanted so badly to think that he didn't want the bullshit anymore, but yet here he was gun pointed at a nigga's face taking his shit. The words N.O. spoke the night he went to his home ran through his head on many nights: *Souljah, until you get shot, you won't really know the meaning to that gun you carry . . .*

"Bruh . . . Take ya finger off the trigger like that. We not here to kill these niggaz!" Zach said, snapping Santana out of thought. Santana shook off his demons he had running through his body. *Damn, blood that will be the death of me,* he thought as he looked Zach fearfully in his eyes. Santana handed Zach the gun.

"If that nigga move, hit son in the face." Santana meant every word and Zach knew it.

"Say no more, shit, I hope you got better luck than me looking around this bitch." Zach trained the gun at the old head's chest.

"As a matter of fact, bitch ass nigga, put ya hands on ya muthafuckin head," Santana said, hate all in his face. Cmore did as he was told without hesitation. He looked at Santana with worry in his eye. Santana's demeanor had changed right before his eyes. He didn't know what that meant for the outcome, but he knew one thing: he wasn't trying to die. Santana began searching under the bed that Cmore sat on. Their minds were different because without even knowing, he knew they searched the dumbest places possible in the home. Santana knew where he would attempt to keep his money if he had a lot of it. Close to him. Santana stopped looking.

"Son, get up! I can't see all the way under this bitch, my G." Cmore stood reluctantly with his hands still on his head. He walked to a corner where a TV stand sat. Santana lifted the bed in one fluid motion, sitting in up against the wall. He now had better access to the contents that were scattered about. The metal frame that held the mattress off the floor was old, rusted and jagged.

"Yo, son, when the fuck you buy this shit, 1950?" Santana laughed. Under the bed were clothes, food wrappers, shoes boxes and scattered mouse traps. Santana kicked the food bags around to make sure nothing was hidden inside of them. Santana rose to his feet.

"Heem, bring that other nigga in here, my G!" Santana yelled out the room. He waited for a reply. He waited a second and there was none. Santana walked into the living room to see why Haseem didn't answer him back. The sight he saw was funny as hell. He laughed to himself. This nigga a fool. The old head had lost his teeth, his tongue hung out his mouth as he wrestled Haseem into a head lock.

"Son, what the fuck is you out here doing? You out here playing and shit. Now this old nigga got ya dumb ass in a head lock." Santana couldn't help himself. The sight was one of pure comedy.

"Get—this—nigga the—fuck—off—me—Br—" Haseem tried to get out before Santana ran up on the old timer and socked him in his face, dropping him to the ground. Haseem turned on the man and started kicking him in his head.

"Son, chill. We not here for all that extra shit. You said it would be something here, right? Let's find it so we can get the fuck out of here before we do some dumb shit." Santana sighed.

"Now both of you niggaz bring your ass on." Santana couldn't help not to laugh at Haseem skinny ass. Him and Haseem caught eye

contact. Santana smiled. *Yeah, nigga, that old nigga was beating that ass,* he couldn't get the thought out of his head. They walked back into the
bedroom where Zach had Cmore at gun point.

"Now you take ya ass over there please. We not gone hurt you old niggaz unless you make us." He looked at the one specifically that was whooping Haseem's ass only moments prior. "Look at it on the plus side, as long as I don't have the gun in my hands, you are definitely safer."

"He dead ass serious, bruh," Zach said. Santana looked at Haseem and pointed to the closet.

"Blood, look in the closet while I finish looking under this bed." Haseem didn't say nothing; he walked to the closet and began searching furiously. Santana knew he was embarrassed; he could tell by his actions.

"Son, that shit ain't 'bout nothing, get ya head together." Santana needed him to know he didn't look or feel no type of way because he let his guard down. Haseem didn't reply; he nodded and got back to the task at hand. Santana did too. He re-searched the food bags, this time with his hands. He didn't want to miss nothing. He threw them aside one by one until he was done with the trash. He moved the clothes, flipped them inside and out. He moved the boxes of shoes to the side. He wanted to search them thoroughly. It was six boxes in total. Santana sat on the metal springs and opened the first box. The Jordan retro 11's stared back at him. He took the shoes out the box. He searched through the brand new shoes. He didn't find nothing. He searched through each box. When he didn't find anything, he tossed the boxes to the side.

"Bruh, why the fuck y'all got so many cartons of cigarettes? Y'all be in this bitch chain smoking!" Haseem joked.

"Nah, son, break the carton open and see if they too smart for they own good," Santana instructed. Haseem did curiously. Nothing but Newports fell out.

"Tana, check them shoes again, these two niggaz got real jittery when you started popping those boxes open!" Zach stated. Cmore glared at him with fire in his eyes.

"My G, you just seen me check them boxes. The shoes are fresh. Never worn. They still have the paper wrap in the soles and all." Santana still grabbed the box, he didn't want Zach to feel like he was belittling him. He opened the box and searched. Nothing.

"Nah, bruh, look in the shoe. This dude real live got sweat beads on his shit." Zach began to get mad. "Bruh, look inside the damn shoes!" Zach exclaimed angrily.

"Youngster, it's nothing here. You can see that for ya self. Just leave and we won't tell Torrey that this shit ever happened." Torrey was a big fat ass nigga that was from Charleston, but had major ties to Ohio, Detroit, and North Carolina. He was what the city would call a million dollar nigga. Santana never really heard of the name, so it rang no bells in his ears. Even if he did know the man and what he was capable of, it would still be no fear regardless.

"Nigga, fuck Torrey!" Haseem yelled. "Now shut the fuck up before my brother smoke ya bitch ass." Haseem was getting madder by each minute that passed.

"Y'all niggas chill, son. Remember we not here for that. And I thought I was the angry one." Santana laughed; the whole shit had him tripping. It was looking like the lick wasn't about to pan out as they thought. For Zach's satisfaction he took the paper out the front of the shoes. He held it up and showed Zach it was nothing in it. He took the paper out the remaining shoe; he told himself if it was nothing in the remaining shoes he was leaving, but with all of their electronics. He wasn't about to leave empty-handed, nah, that was a dead issue. When he took the paper out the toe of the left shoe, he saw the green of money rolled up. Santana looked up excitedly. He was shocked. There was money in the toe of the Jordan. He pulled the roll of money out. It was wrapped very tightly and rubber banded. He popped the rubber band and fanned the money out. The knot contained all hundred dollar bills.

"I fucking knew it. I told you, nigga!" Zach raised the gun back on the old heads with a newfound hope. He was ready to squeeze if either man moved. Santana grabbed the next box; the right shoe was empty. The left shoe contained another roll of money. Santana went through every single box, finding in each left shoe a roll of money. He put all the money in his pocket and stood.

"Heem, grab a trash bag, son. We taking all these boxes of cigs. It's like twenty cartons in that bitch. We can make more money selling those too. We taking that big screen in the living room too. Need that at the spot." Santana looked around to see what else he could take.

"Don't be petty, youngster. You got what you came for. At least leave me and my partner the cigarettes. We gone need them before we meet our maker. Torrey is going to kill us." Cmore meant every word. Santana ignored his bullshit ass pleas.

"You lucky we don't kill ya old ass," Santana stated seriously. Cmore let it be and remained quiet. Haseem did as he was told and grabbed all the cartons of Newports. Santana grabbed the flat screen, Zach kept the gun trained on the men until the car was loaded.

"Lock them niggaz in the room and let's go!" Santana called from the doorway.

"Sorry, bruh, this shit wasn't personal. Money be the motivation!" Zach said as he closed the door to the bedroom and ran out the house to the awaiting car. Haseem sped off. Gunfire came only seconds later. Haseem hit the corner at an angle; the window shattered. Santana

dipped down, Zach had dropped the gun upon entry. Cmore ran in between the house firing on the speeding car. Santana looked for the gun on the floor board. When he finally found it, he didn't raise his head; he just put his hand out the window and fired back. He just wanted to send flame back to make the old head rethink his heroism. Zach's truck bounced off a few cars in the parking lot before actually getting away. Once they hit the interstate and knew the immense danger was over, they laughed together about the whole situation. The three friends held a bond that was rare to Santana. He had only felt like that for a few people in his life and one was killed by his own hand. He felt like he had Justice and Pee Wee back. He missed his childhood in Melrose.

The robbery that took place that night was no real hit to Torrey's pocket, but would be a major one to his pride and street cred. The law of the land was set and in motion. They would be marked men. It was time to play the game as the king, the king of Charleston. The fate that lay ahead would not only change the course of West Virginia's beloved capital, but it was the beginning of a blood-fueled era. The time had come to play for keep sake. The waters were tainted and bloody. The real question now was, who was trying to get their feet wet?

Santana went out the back door and up the alley to Kat's house. The door was open as he knew it would be; he pulled his Glock and called for Kat.

"Kat, where your sexy ass at, ma?" Santana yelled for Kat. Kat sexy ass appeared at the top of the stair landing. She was dressed in the tightest money green Juicy Couture boy shorts. Santana had a crazy view. He was mesmerized. Kat had her hand on hip with a smug grin on her face.

"Get ya ass up here and tell me where you got these damn cigarettes from." Santana locked the door as he walked up the stairs eyeing her every curve. Kat walked into her room. Kat's room was the first room to the left. When he walked up the stairs, he could briefly see into her room and there were what looked like hundreds of cigarettes laid in neat piles on the floor. Santana walked into the room. *Damn. What the fuck!* There was more cigarettes than he could see laid out. Fuck hundreds, it looked like thousands. Seeing that many cigarettes would for sure make a nigga quit. The smell of the nicotine was overbearing.

"Spray something in this bitch, it smells like a tobacco factory in here. This shit making me sick to my stomach!" Santana joked; he wasn't trying to be an asshole. He was serious all in the same breath. Kat glared at him. She wasn't in the mood to play, not at all.

"Fuck all that shit you talking 'bout, where did you get these cartons of cigarettes from?" Kat demanded to know. She stood in the middle of the room. Her pussy lips were protruding from her shorts. Santana couldn't concentrate on nothing but that. He licked his lips. He was horny.

"Uhmmm, hello? What are you staring at?" She followed his gaze. When she saw what he was looking at, she smiled and took a seat.

She snapped her fingers. He licked his lips some more as he looked her deeply into her eyes.

"I don't understand why it matters. I bought them off a geek for the low," Santana replied nonchalantly.

"Don't fucking lie to me. You're lying. No one in their right mind would have never sold you twenty canons unless you cashed them out, especially ones that's holding 20 ounces of hidden crack inside them. So I ask you again. Where did you take this from?" The sound of the 20 ounces put Santana on alert. Now he knew where that half of brick was. The man didn't fabricate that. They had hit Torrey for 30 bands and a half of brick. Santana smiled. He knew it would probably cost them their lives, but he also knew that it would make them rich.

"You bluffing. Where the they at?" Santana got to business. He didn't need to play any more roles. Kat would see who he truly was. A fucking king. Kat got up and walked to her dresser draw. She opened it and pulled out the Ziploc bag that contained the biggest chunks of crack he had ever seen. His heart began to race at a rapid speed. At that moment he was worried about the hit Torrey put on his head. All he saw was the money that he was about to accumulate.

"Santana." He looked up at her. "So are you going to tell me where you got this from?" She sat back down this time in her beanie bag.

"Okay, so do you want the truth or the semi break down of the truth?"

"Shit, keep it *hundred* with me. I need to know what you done got yourself into."

"Okay, well, have you ever heard of a nigga named Torrey?" Santana asked her.

"Yeah, I've heard of him but don't necessarily deal in his kind of circles. He's supposed to be a million dollar nigga or some shit like that. I don't know so I can't talk on him."

"Well, me, Zach and Haseem ran down on a trap house and banged them for *thirty* and these cigarettes. Earlier today, coming out of Young's, a nigga rode up and told us what he heard we did and blah blah blah. We knew about the *thirty*, but we are now finally finding the half of brick, thanks to you." Kat listened, trying to digest what

Santana just had told her.

"Boy, you are only sixteen. Why can't you run around here and be a damn teenager? Why you go and do some dumb shit like that? Did you not learn ya lesson the first time when you almost died on us. You stressing me out, Tana." Kat put her hands on her head. She rubbed her temple in a circular motion. Kat was definitely stressed to her core.

"No disrespect, ma, you're right I'm only sixteen. That's a fact, but that's just my age and age only. I've done been and lived through the illest shit. I know what I got myself into, I knew what I was doing while I was doing it. To what degree I don't know, but I promise you one thing, I can handle mine." Santana got up and took a seat near Kat. He rubbed her back. She sniffled; she was crying.

"I don't want to lose you, Santana. When I saw you coming through the hospital shot last time, it broke me to my core. I jus . . . I just don't want to be the one to tell Simfany that you're hurt again. Promise me that by any means necessary you are going to stay alive?" Kat looked at Santana with tears running down her face.

"On my soul. I will kill anybody who try me." Santana looked Kat deep into her eyes. He wanted her to know what it was for real. He didn't mention the money that was placed on his head; it was a detail that he would leave out. That one notion would have put her stress through the roof.

"Don't worry, it's going to be okay, I promise," Santana said, knowing that the wolves would be out there lurking for sure. What Charleston didn't know or understand was, they were playing with a nigga also that had nothing to lose but his life. And he held his life to the highest value, so when they come they better come playing for keeps.

Jamel Mitchell

Chapter Sixteen

"What's poppin', Ru?" Kev said as he approached Sasha.

"What's up, lor boy?" Sasha replied, smiling ear to ear. Kev ran up the porch and gave his older sister a hug. It had been a while since he stopped through to show love. His time was consumed with trying to end careers on a daily.

"What's been good with you and momma? Where niecey, at?" Kev asked, wanting to see his demon seed of a niece—Diamond.

"Diamond at her lor friend house, trying be too damn grown. That lor girl seven going on twenty-seven." Sasha shook her head at the thought. Diamond was bad as hell; Kev knew it but was still wrapped around her little beautiful finger.

"Man, she get that spoiled shit from Tez, I swear. She is going to be crazy just like y'all nuts. Watch what I tell you. Speaking about Tez, word around town says he just dropped one of them Shotgun Crip niggaz the other night." Sasha rolled her eyes and waited to hear the excuse about to come out Kevin's mouth. Instead, Kevin laughed. The city of Edgewood talked entirely too much. The irony behind it all was that people talked until someone got snatched for it, then the calm of the quiet regained momentum. He never did get the sequence of the constant bullshit.

"Sis, to be real with you, that lor nigga been on bullshit for the last six months. He wants revenge for what happened to the homies. Don't get me wrong. I do too, but niggaz are really clueless on who killed our team. No one confirmed or claimed their bodies. I just can't fathom a nigga from the opposite side being able to get close enough to kill our whole team. Then what threw me for the loop is how the killer knew where Hood lived. I damn near grew up playing in trees with that nigga and I had no clue where he rested his head. To me, if I'm being honest, none of this shit adds up or makes any sense!" Kev said as he leaned against the wood railing on the porch. Kev looked deep into the country skies. He hadn't been to his mother's house in a long time. The country was peaceful, but for the most part safe. The moment was surreal. He was glad that he took the initiative to move his mother into a decent home she could call hers.

"At the end of the day, Kev, this is the life that you two niggaz choose. I understand how you feel, but in the life you live, bro, emotions will get you killed. I'm not saying go run around shooting people you suspect, but always follow ya gut. Instinct is a feeling of life. Don't let no one change how you feel about anything. Whatever your body feel is law. I love you, momma loves you, Tez loves you. I'll even say ya homies love you, but know and understand this clearly, you are the only person that will make sure a hundred percent fact that you survive. So, yeah, I agree Tez out here on bullshit, the drugs definitely not helping the cause. But that little nigga hurting. And as far as I can see, he making the opposition pay in blood. You make sure you—" Her words were cut short by the hail of gun fire that erupted on the quiet street.

Boc—Boc—tatttt—tat—tattt—tat—Boc—Boc!. When Kev heard the crack of the first shot, he instinctively grabbed for his sister. The shooter was able to get close enough before Kev or Sasha knew what to do. Kevin laid on top of his sister, trying to protect her from all danger. The banister was being shredded by rapid gunfire. The splintered wood flew all over porch. The home was under an assault. His mother's home was under attack. It felt like the bullets would never end. Just as the thought left his head, the car scurried off. Kevin jumped up and pulled his weapon. He hopped off the porch, giving chase to the all-black Dodge Charger. *Boc—Boc—Boc—Boc!* He fired his gun in pure anger as the car fled. "Fuck! Fuck! Fuck!" Kev cursed
on his way back to the porch. When he ran to chase the car, Sasha never moved with him. The puddle of blood that was under her head brought tears to his eyes. These niggaz had killed the love of his life. He walked over and checked her pulse. She was still alive and breathing. Her breathing was labored.

"I got you, sis." Kevin ripped his shirt off and applied pressure to her face where the bullet looked like it entered. He didn't wait to call no ambulance. He picked her fragile body into his arms and carried her to his Green Apple Chevy Caprice. As he was about to pull off, his mother came running out the house screaming and crying hysterically. *Where the fuck she just come from*? He was confused. He was sure he didn't hear her in the house. He shrugged the thought away.

"Hurry up, get in!" He rushed his mother. Mrs. Nancy wasted no time hopping in the back with her daughter.

"What the fuck just happened?" Mrs. Nancy asked, tears flooding her face. She looked down at her daughter and lost it. "Sasha—baby, no—Sasha! No. No. No! Kevin, what happened to my baby?" she cried. She laid Sasha's head on her lap and stroked her hair back and forth. He cried. He couldn't bear it. His heart was crumbling by each second that passed. His mother wasn't making nothing easier. Kev peeled out racing his Caprice down Route 24, trying to beat the reaper to the hospital. Mrs. Nancy wailed. She was deeply wounded.

"Ma, shut the fuck up. Please! I need to get her to the hospital. Chill out, she gone be okay." It sounded more believable coming out his mouth. Though his feelings didn't match his words, he tried to stay optimistic.

"Kevin, what happened?" Mrs. Nancy asked sternly in between tears. Kev weaved back and forth through the traffic-filled highway, his eyes burning from the tears that blurred his vision. He looked through the rear view window at his mother. She was broken. She rocked Sasha back and forth, cradling her daughter's head inside of her hands. Someone probably just killed his sister and knowing that he or his brother might have played a role in the tragedy crushed his soul. *How the fuck am I gonna look at my momma?*

"Baby, please say something, talk to me," Mrs. Nancy pleaded from the back seat.

"I don't know what happened, momma. I came over to pick up Diamond. I had promised to take her shopping this weekend. Me and Sasha just got to kicking it and out of nowhere someone opened fire from the driveway. I tackled Sasha to the ground, but I guess . . ." he looked in the rear view at his mother. It killed him inside. "I guess I was too late," Kevin eventually stated.

"Where is your brother?"

"I don't know that either. Me and Sasha was just talking bout him. Tez got a mind of his own, momma. When he hears about this, the streets will for sure be crying blood. As a matter of fact, call him. Here." He reached into his divider for his phone. Without taking his eyes off the road, he found it; he handed it to his mother. She grabbed it, put the phone on speaker and dialed Tez-Mo's number from memory.

"Hello." Tez answered on the first ring. The music blaring in the background made it hard for them to hear anything Tez said.

"Ma? What's up? Where Kev at?" He sounded high. His words slurred badly.

"Turn ya fucking music off. We can't hear you. Now what you say?"

Tez repeated what he said only seconds earlier.

"Kevin is right here." His mother tried to remain calm. That was short-lived.

"Bitch ass nigga, where the fuck you at?" Kevin had no time for pleasantries. Wasn't shit pleasant.

"Hold on, Ru, with that bullshit you on, shorty. What's good? What's got you—"

"My nigga, miss me with all that Ru shit you talking, shorty. Our muthafuckin' sister just took a bullet to the face because of that dumb shit you did. Bring ya bitch ass to Harford General now. And get every gun we got ready. We 'bout to send niggaz to meet their makers tonight."

"I'm doing that now, then I'm on my way. Man, fuck! Is Sasha going to be okay, bro? Is Sasha alive, Kev?" Tez-Mo asked as he cried on the other end of the phone.

"She holding on, baby. Do what ya brother asked you to do, then bring ya ass to the hospital. You hear me? I love you, baby, and no matter what your brother says, this isn't your fault. Calm yourself and get to your family. We need you more than ever right now." Mrs. Nancy replied in the calmest of tone possible. Her boys were just like their daddy. They all acted off of bad vibes and exerted energy. She needed him to make it to the hospital without getting himself killed or killing someone else. That could be done on a later date.

"Okay," was all he said before he hung up the phone. Kevin pulled into the hospital after what felt like the longest ten minutes in history. Kevin pulled on to the curb of the emergency entrance, only inches away to the sliding doors. He rushed from the driver side to the back where his mother held Sasha's limb body. Mrs. Nancy ran in front of him yelling for help.

"Somebody, help! She's been shot in the head." Mrs. Nancy didn't need to yell again. Three doctors and a gurney came out of nowhere to assist Sasha. Kev tried to follow them as they rushed to the back, but was stopped by the security guard on duty. He couldn't go no further. His sister's fate was in the hands of Allah—the all-knowing, the all-forgiving. Kev walked back to the waiting room and sat near his mother. She held him. Finally, Kevin let his emotions flood through his body. Kevin wiped his face, he looked his mother in her eyes and said:

"As soon as Tez gets here I'ma leave you to handle this and I'll be back shortly either to wait on the outcome of the surgery or to be fitted for a body bag. Niggaz will pay dearly for this. On grandma someone will pay for this." Kev rocked his mother back and forth, while he rubbed her back up and down at an attempt to soothe her pain.

***

Santana walked into the room and smiled. Zach and Haseem no longer looked depressed. 'Bout damn time. Santana still hadn't told them about the situation with Kat and the 20 ounces. Well, the 18 now because he told Kat that she could keep the other two for herself. She was reluctant at first. But he explained that he would buy them back from her if she wanted to sell them. It wasn't like she was gone hit the block with them anyway. In all reality she was just holding it for him until he was ready to fuck with it. She had an option. He could have cashed her then and there or wait until she needed the money and sell them then. He wanted to bless her in more ways than one. She could have kept the 20 ounces to herself but she didn't. He loved her for her loyalty.

Zach and Haseem stayed in the house mopping around every-where, scared to death to leave the house. What Santana found so hilarious was that Moca didn't even want shit to do with them niggas. Santana sat the food down on the bed. They all needed to put some food on their stomachs. Santana was really the only one still making sure shit got done.

"What's good, son? I see y'all bounced back to life a little bit. So are we ready to talk about this shit or do we keep entertaining this big ass elephant running around this bitch?" Santana asked, opening the Chinese food. He pulled some chicken wings out and ate them.

"Fuck what you talking 'bout, pass that food. That shit smell good as shit!" Haseem replied, reaching for the Chinese food also. Zach followed suit. They were both hungry as hell. How they smashed them chicken wings was carnivorous. *Damn, these niggas look like they haven't eaten in weeks. What the flack!* Santana laughed as he watched Zach eat the wing bone dry. They all ate until they were on a full stomach. Now it was time to address the bullshit in the room.

"Good looking, bruh. We was in this bitch losing pounds!" Zach said, licking his fingers with Moca at his feet.

"You want some chicken too, girl? Here." Santana pulled a few chicken wings out and gave them to her.

"You know you fucked up doing that, right? Now she gone be at your feet!" Zach confirmed.

"I'm straight with it. But on a real note, we have some shit that can't hold off no more. I need your undivided attention. Am I asking too much?" Santana stretched. That food put a hurting on him. He was growing tired.

"You not asking for too much. It's 'bout time we spoke on the shit now anyway." Zach agreed.

"Ain't really shit to speak about. Niggaz want our heads, period!" Haseem said sarcastically.

"My nigga, why do I feel like you have an issue with us about some shit you planned. So what's ya issue, blood, because when we split that thirty bands three ways and this half of brick you ain't have no problem. So now the nigga Torrey speaking 'bout dropping us over it and it's a fucking problem." Santana was beginning to get tired of Haseem acting like a bitch. He had been acting like a hoe ever since they left Young's Department store. "What happened to that *The-World-Is-Ours* bullshit you was screaming only days ago?" Santana burst out laughing. He was trying to lighten the mood. Zach tried to remain serious but Santana was just too silly. Haseem even smiled.

He knew that Santana meant no harm in his words. Haseem knew what he was saying was truth.

"Blood, we never split a half of brick. I don't know where they keep getting that shit from." Zach was starting to get mad that they fucked up and left a half of brick in the dope house. Santana said nothing further. He pulled the Nike sports bag off his back and dumped the contents on the bed. On the bed were multiple guns he bought from fiends that were willing to trade for crack. And the Zip loc bag that held the half of birdie. The look on their face was priceless.

"What's that look for? You thought ya brother was running around fucking hoes and eating Gino's? My life flashed across my eyes too, my G. I wasn't trying to be sitting here day dreaming and wiggling my thumbs, hoping this shit disappears. We here now. The question is, how are we going to handle this shit? Now that I have your attention, hear me, shorty. Them cigarettes we gave Kat had the bag hidden in them. It was really twenty ounces, but I told her to keep two for herself for keep-it-a-stack-with-me. In all honesty, I had to force her to take payment. I bought us more guns; so, as Haseem said before, I'm not the only one running round here flamed up. We have three Glock 26's. Those are the 9 millimeters. A .357 Ruger and this Tech . . . I think it's a 9 also. I got one vest. That's for whoever feels they need it the most. More to come on those. Or so I'm being told. All I want is one of the Glocks. I already have the one Smith 'n' Wesson. That'll leave us with two hammers apiece. Zach, I got the .357 for you. Your hands the only ones big enough to hold a cannon of that caliber. But it's on y'all how you niggaz bust them bitches down."

Santana grabbed one on the glizzys off the bed.

"So you thought of all the stops, I see," Haseem added, impressed.

"Nah, my G. I thought of all the ways to put us in the game, making our chances of survival greater. And as I said last time, I don't want just any nigga thinking we sweet. So my advice to you both—bust them guns at all cost. Be aggressive with ya shit. I promise it will keep
you alive. Always remember don't nobody wants to die. And that's on both sides of the spectrum. If the opposition see weakness when

them cannons begin to go off, everyone and their momma gone want a shot at that fifteen bands. They will look at it how I would look at it; it's free money. Which is why we have to prove difference. We gone show these niggaz our guns bust too, and more efficiently. When they come, they better come correct. Once we establish these guidelines, you'll see how these pussy ass niggas tend to lift their skirts. Moving on." Zach and Haseem's face was that of pure admiration. Santana smiled inside. They were finally listening. Santana was talking survival and they needed all the tools to do just that. *Survive.*

"Why y'all sitting over there looking at me like that?"

"No reason, bruh, just sound like you know what you talking about. Sounds like the words of someone that snatched a soul or two before. The strategizing is too natural, the planning is too precise and the way you talk has meaning behind each word. The fear of the unknown will always be there, for us at least. You seem so nonchalant about the whole situation. I seen a glimpse of how you bring shit and to be honest I'm just glad you on this side, bruh. I love you, my nigga. That shit resides in ya eyes. We gone set this shit off, ain't we bruh?" Zach asked, excitedly holding the newly bought .357 Ruger in his hand.

"He right, bruh, you on some G.I. Joe shit tonight," Haseem clowned.

"To be truthful, as long as it keeps us living, I'm with whatever. Try to make minimal mistakes, please, because we all are accountable for our own. And I don't want to become a memory over yours. Especially ones that can be avoided with common sense. So again try to make as little as possible. Now here are six ounces apiece. I only took four for myself because I had to buy the guns and body armor. Make your money, but be careful. We can try to mob with each other for a few days, but eventually that will get old. If two of us are together, then it's only right the other man takes the vest. Agreed?" Santana looked up for their approval. They both nodded in agreement. "A'ight, bet." Santana went into Zach's closet and grabbed the sandwich bags that contained their cut. Santana pulled the scale out of his pocket to weigh the yay. "My nigga, what you doing?" Haseem asked, offended.

"What the fuck it look like, my G?" Santana was lost; it was obvious what he was doing. "What type of—"

"My nigga, you called us to tell us you had six free ounces for us and you think you have to still put it on the scale? For what? We are appreciative, my nigga. You good money, bruh. We love you. That ain't needed. If it's short a few grams here or there, my nigga, the love make up for it. On blood. Thank you, bruh, you are the epitome of a brother." Zach meant every word spoken. He had never met anyone like Santana. He was humble, loyal, and ready for whatever.

"I appreciate the love my nigga, and I love you niggaz too, son. I'm never too old to learn new shit. You showed me how to chop, cook, and eye this work. It's only right that I do good business. It was just by habit, bruh, my bad." He laughed. "And for the record, this shit came with a price. We just don't know at what cost yet."

"You right," Zach said in agreement. "Fuck Torrey. We real kings. Watch, we gone show these niggaz." Zach stood aiming the .357 at the mirror. The gun made him feel like God in a sense. At that moment he was ready to take a soul.

"Sit ya dumb ass down before you pop one of us by mistake!" Haseem exclaimed. He wasn't with being in the room while guns were being waved around, especially for no reason at all. That was a death wish. He knew all across the country kids were being killed mistakenly, by a friend's carelessness. He promised he wouldn't go out like that.

"Bruh, ain't no bullets in them, I made sure of that because I knew one of you muthafuckas was gone do some dumb shit just like Zach doing right now. It's the power that the gun gives you. My nigga, sit the fuck down, you making son nervous. But for real, y'all better get sharp with these bitches, ya life will one day eventually depend on it." Santana reached into the Nike sports bag and pulled out enough ammo to damn near to start a war with a small army.

"My nigga thought of all the angles to this shit," Zach said out loud, taking a hand full of .357 shells. Haseem grabbed a hand full for his Glock's also.

"And they hollows," Haseem added. He was excited. He knew the damage those bullets would cause. He dropped the loose bullets and took a box.

"Now wipe all those bullets off with ya thirsty ass. You have to be more careful than that, Heem, damn. Use these gloves, wipe down what you already touched then load ya weapons. Never ever ever ever touch these bullets with ya bare palms. Stop acting like y'all stupid. If you wanna go to jail after you escape death, shit, be my guests, just don't drag me in that bitch with you. My only words of advice are if you pull it, use it. Don't let niggaz slide, for real. Another thing—I won't speak about none of this unless we are in person. I love y'all, son. Time to—"

"Play for keeps!" Zach and Haseem said in unison. Santana said that phrase so much they knew it was coming. It was crazy how much they knew him already. Santana was just about to talk shit, but was cut short due to the ringing of his phone. His mother's picture popped up. Santana sighed; he didn't know what to expect from this conversation. He answered.

"Pretty lady . . ." he spoke the familiar words.

"What you been doing with yourself?" Simfany asked. She missed him dearly. The last time they talked, she was getting in his ass about using drugs and lacking.

"Been good, ma, now isn't the time to talk. I'm kind of busy. Can I call you back in a few? We have a lot that needs to be said anyway." That was his way of telling her he was around ears.

"Okay, I love you, make sure you call me back in a few hours tops. You hear me?" Simfany stated firmly.

"I love you too, pretty lady, and I promise to hit you back when I am able to," Santana assured her.

"Okay, papi. I love you, Tana."

"Love you too, ma," Santana replied back and slid his Sidekick back into place. The conversation went better than he expected. His mind was at ease knowing that his mother wasn't no longer disgusted with him. Back to the task at hand, Santana put a set of latex gloves on and took the .9 millimeter bullets out the box. He proceeded to stack the double clip for his Glock .26 compact edition. The thoughts, as he loaded his weapon, were grim. He was confident in his murder game, but he wasn't 100% confident in shit else. Especially not in Zach and Haseem. They meant well, but how far were they willing to go? He didn't know. He for sure couldn't bet his life on it. Santana was not trying to let the streets of Charleston claim his soul. He told himself over and over that his soul would never disconnect from his body in Charleston, West Virginia or any other city for that matter. One thing he knew for sure, two things for certain; he would not sleep on the men and women that prowled in the city streets. He refused to succumb to a demise. His or his friends'. If they wanted to claim his body, the killers better come correct. Survival was at all cost. One thing Santana knew for sure: He was a muthfuckin' survivor.

***

Tez-Mo pulled into the parking lot of Harford County General Hospital recklessly. The smell of marijuana reeked from his green and black Yukon truck. Tez-Mo pulled his visor down and looked in his mirror. *Damn, my nigga, you looking rough.* The combination of weed, codeine and liquor had Tez-Mo looking insane and wild. His hair was everywhere, his eyes were bloodshot, and his hands was shaking uncontrollably. He hated what stared back at him. The news of his baby sister being shot only tore him down more mentally and emotionally. Tez-Mo wiped the falling tears from his eyes. He took the XD .45 Springfield off his hip and put it under the driver seat. He looked at himself again and made sure he looked presentable. He exited his truck and walked into the hospital.

Tez-Mo looked around for his mother and his brother; he didn't see no one. He walked around the hospital in search of his family. He couldn't find them nowhere. He walked through the shuffling people in the lobby of the hospital's location station.

"Excuse me, ma'am, I'm looking for directions to the room for my sister—Sasha Brooks." The pretty brown-eyed nurse looked up at Tez-Mo.

"Do you know what floor she could be on?" the nurse asked as she looked Tez-Mo up and down. It was a questionable look Tez-Mo could tell.

"Nah, I just know she got shot a few hours ago. My little brother and my mother rushed her in here by car," Tez-Mo tried to explain.

"Do you have a medical power of attorney card?" the nurse asked.

"Fuck are you talking about, shorty? Nah, I don't have no fucking medical power shit. Where the fuck is my lor sister, my nigga! All this extra shit is for the birds. Where the fuck is my fucking sister!" He began to get irate.

"Please calm down, there is a policy in place that only allows us to tell you about your family if you have a medical power of attorney. The security of hospitals have risen." The nurse tried to explain. Tez-Mo wasn't hearing none of it.

"You playing, right? So you telling me if your muthafuckin sister got shot in her muthafuckin' head, it would be alright for me to tell you to fuck off?" Tez wiped the sweat from his forehead.

"Sir, it's not my—" Tez leaned closer to her.

"Listen, bitch, where the fuck is my sister at? And I'm not flicking playing with you!" Tez-Mo's eyes were bloodshot from the mixed drugs he had in his body. He was slipping. The one thing he preached to his brother, he began to fall victim to. Between the drugs, his appearance and mixed emotions, he had the nurse looking at him in pure terror. The nurse typed on her computer against her better judgment. Tez-Mo sighed in relief.

"Thank you, sweetheart." The nurse looked up but said nothing. She could understand how he felt. The information that popped up on the screen was not only sad, but was most likely going to set Tez-Mo off if she relayed it to him. So, instead, she gave him the room number that Sasha Brooks still occupied. She wasn't going to be the one to tell him that his sister was deceased.

"Sir, it says here that she is supposed to be in *Room 5* in the ICU wing," she said reluctantly.

"Thank you." Tez-Mo knocked on the counter and took off down the corridor to the ICU unit. She watched as Tez-Mo ran down the corridor; her heart went out to the family. To die in such conditions was not only heartbreaking but senseless. The nurse looked back to the computer; she finished reading the report that the doctor entered into the database about Sasha Brooks:

Gunshot Victim, Female, 19 years old, drive by shooting.
Shot once in the face, neck and chest.
Brain dead on arrival. Pronounced deceased at 4:15 p.m.
End of report

The nurse shook her head at the tragedy. She closed the file and exited to the main page and said a silent prayer for the loved ones of Sasha Brooks.

When Tez finally gained entrance to the fifth room in the ICU wing, he stood in confusion. There was no one there. Not his little brother or his mother. He walked into the room. He could see Sasha laying there helplessly. The tears that ran from his eyes were of guilt. He was the reason that she was laying hurt in a hospital. He made his way to the bedside and sat down in the chair. He sat and held his sister's hand. Tez-Mo rocked back and forth with anger.

"Whoever did this, Sash, they're going to pay. I promise, beauty!" Tez-Mo cried. He was hurt; they had finally hit where it hurt most. His heart. He rubbed her hand in circular motions as he mumbled to his self. Something felt odd to him as he sat there. He couldn't exactly pin point it, but something wasn't right. He didn't hear no monitors beeping; it was an eerie silence in the room. He looked up; the heart monitor was off, there was no IV bag in his sister's arm. He rose from the chair and walked to the doctor's station.

"Excuse me, I'm trying to understand why my sister's heart monitor is off," Tez-Mo said calmly.

"What room are you referring to, sir?" the male doctor asked inquisitively. He looked back at the room he just left from.

"Room 5—Sasha Brooks is the name of the patient." The doctor looked into the eyes of the young man. He could see heartbreak as well as indication of substance abuse.

"Give me one second please." The doctor got on the phone and called security. He knew he most likely would need them. The young man would probably need to be subdued. The doctor prolonged for a few minutes; he was going to wait until the officer came. Tez-Mo leaned against the counter waiting on the doctor to return. When he saw the officers come through the door, he looked up for the doctor. He began to put two and two together in his drug-induced brain. "Tell me what's going on, doc!" Tez demanded. "I'm sorry, son, Sasha Brooks was pronounced dead at 4:15, sir. She came into the ICU with your mother and brother, I assume?" Tez just nodded. "She came in brain dead from the shot to her face." He looked at the computer and strolled down. "A Ms. Nancy Brooks pulled the plug on the respirator. Your sister had no chance of living through the night. The only reason we left her in there this long is because your mother asked that we let you see her before we took her to the morgue. I'm very, very sorry sir." Tez-Mo just walked off and went back into the room with his sister where she laid dead to the world. He just looked at her and he couldn't find the words. Apologizing would never be enough. The person that help him raise Kev when their momma ran to the streets was gone. His heart was gone forever. He cried, he cried hard. The pain was so unbearable, he didn't know how he could look his mother in the eyes after this. He walked closer to the hospital bed to face Sasha. He needed to see her beautiful face. He hadn't cried like this since a child.

"Sis, I know sorry isn't enough. But I'm so so sorry for this. I know being forgiven for this can never happen. Truthfully, I don't think I can ever forgive myself. I love you with all my heart and on mommy I will send people ya way for this. I can see you shaking ya head about
that, but baby, I can't let that go down like that. Please forgive me, sis, for the terror I'm 'bout to cause in ya name. I promise to take care of our baby girl Diamond, momma and Kevin. I love you, sis. I'm sorry—I'm sorry!" he cried deeply. "I love you, beautiful. May Allah have mercy upon your soul." Tez-Mo leaned forward and kissed her cheek, then her hand. He rubbed her hand as he slowly tucked it in her bed.

"I love you, Sasha Momma." Tez-Mo put his hand over his heart as he backed out of the room. The doctor's heart went out to the young man. Tez-Mo walked out the hospital with blurred vision. The tears blinded him as he walked slowly back to his car. He was glad that he left his gun under his car seat, because the kind of anger he held within him, he might have crashed out on the wrong cause. When he closed the door to his car, he yelled at the top of his lungs and pounded the steering wheel repeatedly.

"Fuck! Fuck! Fuck! Fuck! God, why? God, why?" He braced his head on the steering wheel and cried deep and long. His heart was shattered gravely. He wiped his eyes, put his truck in *drive* and sped out the parking lot. Somebody was going to die tonight; Tez-Mo was going to make sure of that. He needed to gather his thoughts and talk to his brother. He wasn't trying to do some dumb shit. But before the night was over, the reaper would claim the life of someone from the other side. And how he looked at it now, all was fair in war. There were no boundaries that couldn't be crossed or limitations one could go to bring blood. Everybody could get it. All was fair game. No rules to abide by. Women and children were now plates waiting to be eaten.

***

The nurse wiped her tears away as she watched Tez-Mo blindly leaving the hospital's entrance. She felt the pain that flowed from his body. She shook her head at the anguish. She hoped he would go seek justice by way of the land. She knew that if someone killed her, she would want her brother, husband or father to send her killer with her. Again she prayed for the family of the fallen, but this time she put angels over Tez-Mo in his mission for revenge.

***

Drew poured gasoline over the Dodge Charger. The stolen car did what he needed it to do. He didn't get to confirm his kill, but as many bullets as he shot from his modified AK-47, he knew a soul left to be with God that night. He sparked his blunt and pulled on it. The sour diesel hit his lungs hard and tastefully. He inhaled deeply, closing his eyes in the process. His burner phone buzzed. He had a text message from one his closest Loc homies. The message was sweet and simple. It read: *CONFIRMED*. It was the message that indicated a body was dropped. He smiled took another pull from his blunt and threw the blunt into the seat of the vehicle. He walked off and jumped into the passenger seat of the awaiting car.

"How that shit make you feel, cuz?" the driver asked.

"How what make me feel, cuz?" Drew asked in response.

"To have ya first confirmed kill, shorty," the man said excitedly for him.

"Shit, Loc, it won't be my first for long. You hear me, shorty?" Drew assured.

"Who else you got on ya agenda?" the man asked, putting his hand on the gear shift to leave from behind the abandoned warehouse.

"You, my nigga." Drew already had his gun raised to Ty's temple.

"Cuz, what I do?" Ty pleaded, knowing his days on earth were over.

"Tell Kane I send my love, you bitch ass nigga." He fired, ending his life once and for all. He kicked Ty's body out the car. He moved into the driver seat and rolled the window down to conceal the blood splatter. Once all evidence of foul play was handled, he put the car in gear and sped off. The love he possessed for Ty was superficial. When he came home and heard about him taking off on Kane during his murder, he knew that he would end his life. He lived by a different code of life. Death before dishonor was a real thing to him. He labeled Ty a coward and in his line of work, that was punishable by death.

***

"Oh my god! Remy, hurry the fuck up. I don't have all damn day!" Nessy complained. She threw her phone on the couch and pouted as if Remy could see her. Her phone rang. She answered it.

"What? You always playing. I told you that I wanted some dick. If you not going to come over here, then say that shit then." Nessy was pissed.

"Ma, I'll be there in a few minutes. I'm on the West handling some shit for Von," Remy assured her.

"Yeah, like you always say. You might as well start fucking Von. Bitch ass nigga! I'm over this shit with you." She hung up again. Nessy turned her phone off, she wasn't trying to be bothered now.

Nessy went into the bathroom and started a hot bath; she needed to relax. She could fuck herself. She went into her room in search of her favorite dildo, but was interrupted by a knock on her door.

"Ahhhhh—I swear to God!" Nessy screamed in frustration.

"Who is it?" she said, walking to the door. She looked through the peep hole. It was black. The person on the other end had their finger over it.

"Stop playing. Who the fuck is it?" she tried looking again.

"Really?" was all the other person said in a hushed tone. She smiled. Finally, he had arrived.

"Remy, you play too much." Nessy unlocked the door and opened it. Her smile faded when she saw who was on the other side of the door. He wore a mask but by his build she knew who he was and what he was there to do. Nessy tried to sprint back into her house. The man raised his gun and fired into her back, dropping her instantly. Nessy crawled to the kitchen trying to escape her killer.

"Please, I swear. I'm sorry. Please don't kill me!" Nessy cried.

"See you in hell," he said with the biggest smirk on his face.

"Fatty Man—Nooooooooooooooo!" Nessy tried to cover her face, but the bullets ripped through her body ferociously, sending her soul to its maker for the rest of eternity.

To Be Continued...
For The Love of Blood 4
Coming Soon

Lock Down Publications and Ca$h Presents assisted publishing packages.

BASIC PACKAGE $499
Editing
Cover Design
Formatting

UPGRADED PACKAGE $800
Typing
Editing
Cover Design
Formatting

ADVANCE PACKAGE $1,200
Typing
Editing
Cover Design
Formatting
Copyright registration
Proofreading
Upload book to Amazon

LDP SUPREME PACKAGE $1,500
Typing
Editing
Cover Design
Formatting
Copyright registration
Proofreading
Set up Amazon account
Upload book to Amazon
Advertise on LDP Amazon and Facebook page

***Other services available upon request. Additional charges may apply
Lock Down Publications
P.O. Box 944
Stockbridge, GA 30281-9998
Phone # 470 303-9761

Submission Guideline

Submit the first three chapters of your completed manuscript to ldpsubmissions@gmail.com, subject line: Your book's title. The manuscript must be in a .doc file and sent as an attachment. Document should be in Times New Roman, double spaced and in size 12 font. Also, provide your synopsis and full contact information. If sending multiple submissions, they must each be in a separate email.

Have a story but no way to send it electronically? You can still submit to LDP/Ca$h Presents. Send in the first three chapters, written or typed, of your completed manuscript to:

LDP: Submissions Dept
Po Box 944
Stockbridge, Ga 30281

DO NOT send original manuscript. Must be a duplicate.

Provide your synopsis and a cover letter containing your full contact information.

Thanks for considering LDP and Ca$h Presents.

<u>NEW RELEASES</u>

IT'S JUST ME AND YOU 2 by AH'MILLION

SOUL OF A HUSTLER, HEART OF A KILLER 3 by SAYNO-MORE

THE COCAINE PRINCESS 9 by KING RIO

FOR THE LOVE OF BLOOD 3 by JAMEL MITCHELL

STRAIGHT BEAST MODE III

De'Kari

KINGPIN KILLAZ IV

STREET KINGS III

PAID IN BLOOD III

CARTEL KILLAZ IV

DOPE GODS III

Hood Rich

SINS OF A HUSTLA II

ASAD

YAYO V

Bred In The Game 2

S. Allen

THE STREETS WILL TALK II

By Yolanda Moore

SON OF A DOPE FIEND III

HEAVEN GOT A GHETTO III

SKI MASK MONEY III

By Renta

LOYALTY AIN'T PROMISED III

By Keith Williams

I'M NOTHING WITHOUT HIS LOVE II

SINS OF A THUG II

TO THE THUG I LOVED BEFORE II

IN A HUSTLER I TRUST II

By Monet Dragun

QUIET MONEY IV

EXTENDED CLIP III

THUG LIFE IV

By **Trai'Quan**

Jamel Mitchell

THE STREETS MADE ME IV
By **Larry D. Wright**
IF YOU CROSS ME ONCE III
ANGEL V
By **Anthony Fields**
THE STREETS WILL NEVER CLOSE IV
By **K'ajji**
HARD AND RUTHLESS III
KILLA KOUNTY IV
By Khufu
MONEY GAME III
By Smoove Dolla
JACK BOYS VS DOPE BOYS IV
A GANGSTA'S QUR'AN V
COKE GIRLZ II
COKE BOYS II
LIFE OF A SAVAGE V
CHI'RAQ GANGSTAS V
SOSA GANG IV
BRONX SAVAGES II
BODYMORE KINGPINS II
BLOOD OF A GOON II
By Romell Tukes
MURDA WAS THE CASE III
Elijah R. Freeman
AN UNFORESEEN LOVE IV
BABY, I'M WINTERTIME COLD III
By **Meesha**

QUEEN OF THE ZOO III

For the Love of Blood

By **Black Migo**
CONFESSIONS OF A JACKBOY III
By Nicholas Lock
KING KILLA II
By Vincent "Vitto" Holloway
BETRAYAL OF A THUG III
By Fre$h
THE BIRTH OF A GANGSTER III
By Delmont Player
TREAL LOVE II
By Le'Monica Jackson
FOR THE LOVE OF BLOOD IV
By Jamel Mitchell
RAN OFF ON DA PLUG II
By Paper Boi Rari
HOOD CONSIGLIERE III
By Keese
PRETTY GIRLS DO NASTY THINGS II
By Nicole Goosby
LOVE IN THE TRENCHES II
By Corey Robinson
FOREVER GANGSTA III
By Adrian Dulan
THE COCAINE PRINCESS X
SUPER GREMLIN II
By King Rio
CRIME BOSS II
Playa Ray
LOYALTY IS EVERYTHING III
Molotti

Jamel Mitchell

HERE TODAY GONE TOMORROW II
By Fly Rock
REAL G'S MOVE IN SILENCE II
By Von Diesel
GRIMEY WAYS IV
By Ray Vinci
SALUTE MY SAVAGERY II
By Fumiya Payne
BLOOD AND GAMES II
By King Dream

Available Now

RESTRAINING ORDER **I & II**
By **CA$H & Coffee**
LOVE KNOWS NO BOUNDARIES **I II & III**
By **Coffee**
RAISED AS A GOON I, II, III & IV
BRED BY THE SLUMS I, II, III
BLAST FOR ME I & II
ROTTEN TO THE CORE I II III
A BRONX TALE I, II, III
DUFFLE BAG CARTEL I II III IV V VI
HEARTLESS GOON I II III IV V
A SAVAGE DOPEBOY I II
DRUG LORDS I II III

For the Love of Blood

CUTTHROAT MAFIA I II
KING OF THE TRENCHES
By **Ghost**
LAY IT DOWN **I & II**
LAST OF A DYING BREED I II
BLOOD STAINS OF A SHOTTA I & II III
By **Jamaica**
LOYAL TO THE GAME I II III
LIFE OF SIN I, II III
By **TJ & Jelissa**
BLOODY COMMAS I & II
SKI MASK CARTEL I II & III
KING OF NEW YORK I II,III IV V
RISE TO POWER I II III
COKE KINGS I II III IV V
BORN HEARTLESS I II III IV
KING OF THE TRAP I II
By **T.J. Edwards**
IF LOVING HIM IS WRONG…I & II
LOVE ME EVEN WHEN IT HURTS I II III
By **Jelissa**
WHEN THE STREETS CLAP BACK I & II III
THE HEART OF A SAVAGE I II III IV
MONEY MAFIA I II
LOYAL TO THE SOIL I II III
By **Jibril Williams**
A DISTINGUISHED THUG STOLE MY HEART I II & III
LOVE SHOULDN'T HURT I II III IV
RENEGADE BOYS I II III IV
PAID IN KARMA I II III

Jamel Mitchell

SAVAGE STORMS I II III

AN UNFORESEEN LOVE I II III

BABY, I'M WINTERTIME COLD I II

By **Meesha**

A GANGSTER'S CODE I &, II III

A GANGSTER'S SYN I II III

THE SAVAGE LIFE I II III

CHAINED TO THE STREETS I II III

BLOOD ON THE MONEY I II III

A GANGSTA'S PAIN I II III

By J-Blunt

PUSH IT TO THE LIMIT

By **Bre' Hayes**

BLOOD OF A BOSS **I, II, III, IV, V**

SHADOWS OF THE GAME

TRAP BASTARD

By **Askari**

THE STREETS BLEED MURDER **I, II & III**

THE HEART OF A GANGSTA I II& III

By **Jerry Jackson**

CUM FOR ME I II III IV V VI VII VIII

An **LDP Erotica Collaboration**

BRIDE OF A HUSTLA **I II & II**

THE FETTI GIRLS **I, II& III**

CORRUPTED BY A GANGSTA I, II III, IV

BLINDED BY HIS LOVE

THE PRICE YOU PAY FOR LOVE I, II ,III

DOPE GIRL MAGIC I II III

By **Destiny Skai**

WHEN A GOOD GIRL GOES BAD

For the Love of Blood

By **Adrienne**

THE COST OF LOYALTY I II III

By Kweli

A GANGSTER'S REVENGE **I II III & IV**

THE BOSS MAN'S DAUGHTERS I II III IV V

A SAVAGE LOVE **I & II**

BAE BELONGS TO ME I II

A HUSTLER'S DECEIT I, II, III

WHAT BAD BITCHES DO I, II, III

SOUL OF A MONSTER I II III

KILL ZONE

A DOPE BOY'S QUEEN I II III

TIL DEATH

By **Aryanna**

A KINGPIN'S AMBITON

A KINGPIN'S AMBITION **II**

I MURDER FOR THE DOUGH

By **Ambitious**

TRUE SAVAGE I II III IV V VI VII

DOPE BOY MAGIC I, II, III

MIDNIGHT CARTEL I II III

CITY OF KINGZ I II

NIGHTMARE ON SILENT AVE

THE PLUG OF LIL MEXICO II

CLASSIC CITY

By **Chris Green**

A DOPEBOY'S PRAYER

By **Eddie "Wolf" Lee**

THE KING CARTEL **I, II & III**

By **Frank Gresham**

THESE NIGGAS AIN'T LOYAL **I, II & III**
By **Nikki Tee**
GANGSTA SHYT **I II &III**
By **CATO**
THE ULTIMATE BETRAYAL
By **Phoenix**
BOSS'N UP **I , II & III**
By **Royal Nicole**
I LOVE YOU TO DEATH
By **Destiny J**
I RIDE FOR MY HITTA
I STILL RIDE FOR MY HITTA
By **Misty Holt**
LOVE & CHASIN' PAPER
By **Qay Crockett**
TO DIE IN VAIN
SINS OF A HUSTLA
By **ASAD**
BROOKLYN HUSTLAZ
By **Boogsy Morina**
BROOKLYN ON LOCK I & II
By **Sonovia**
GANGSTA CITY
By **Teddy Duke**
A DRUG KING AND HIS DIAMOND I & II III
A DOPEMAN'S RICHES
HER MAN, MINE'S TOO I, II
CASH MONEY HO'S
THE WIFEY I USED TO BE I II
PRETTY GIRLS DO NASTY THINGS

For the Love of Blood

By Nicole Goosby
TRAPHOUSE KING **I II & III**
KINGPIN KILL'AZ I II III
STREET KINGS I II
PAID IN BLOOD **I II**
CARTEL KILLAZ I II III
DOPE GODS I II
By **Hood Rich**
LIPSTICK KILLAH **I, II, III**
CRIME OF PASSION I II & III
FRIEND OR FOE I II III
By **Mimi**
STEADY MOBBN' **I, II, III**
THE STREETS STAINED MY SOUL I II III
By **Marcellus Allen**
WHO SHOT YA **I, II, III**
SON OF A DOPE FIEND I II
HEAVEN GOT A GHETTO I II
SKI MASK MONEY I II
Renta
GORILLAZ IN THE BAY **I II III IV**
TEARS OF A GANGSTA I II
3X KRAZY I II
STRAIGHT BEAST MODE I II
DE'KARI
TRIGGADALE I II III
MURDAROBER WAS THE CASE I II
Elijah R. Freeman
GOD BLESS THE TRAPPERS I, II, III
THESE SCANDALOUS STREETS I, II, III

Jamel Mitchell

FEAR MY GANGSTA I, II, III IV, V

THESE STREETS DON'T LOVE NOBODY I, II

BURY ME A G I, II, III, IV, V

A GANGSTA'S EMPIRE I, II, III, IV

THE DOPEMAN'S BODYGAURD I II

THE REALEST KILLAZ I II III

THE LAST OF THE OGS I II III

Tranay Adams

THE STREETS ARE CALLING

Duquie Wilson

MARRIED TO A BOSS I II III

By Destiny Skai & Chris Green

KINGZ OF THE GAME I II III IV V VI VII

CRIME BOSS

Playa Ray

SLAUGHTER GANG I II III

RUTHLESS HEART I II III

By Willie Slaughter

FUK SHYT

By Blakk Diamond

DON'T F#CK WITH MY HEART I II

By Linnea

ADDICTED TO THE DRAMA I II III

IN THE ARM OF HIS BOSS II

By Jamila

YAYO I II III IV

A SHOOTER'S AMBITION I II

BRED IN THE GAME

By S. Allen

TRAP GOD I II III

194

For the Love of Blood

RICH $AVAGE I II III
MONEY IN THE GRAVE I II III
By Martell Troublesome Bolden
FOREVER GANGSTA I II
GLOCKS ON SATIN SHEETS I II
By Adrian Dulan
TOE TAGZ I II III IV
LEVELS TO THIS SHYT I II
IT'S JUST ME AND YOU I II
By Ah'Million
KINGPIN DREAMS I II III
RAN OFF ON DA PLUG
By Paper Boi Rari
CONFESSIONS OF A GANGSTA I II III IV
CONFESSIONS OF A JACKBOY I II
By Nicholas Lock
I'M NOTHING WITHOUT HIS LOVE
SINS OF A THUG
TO THE THUG I LOVED BEFORE
A GANGSTA SAVED XMAS
IN A HUSTLER I TRUST
By Monet Dragun
CAUGHT UP IN THE LIFE I II III
THE STREETS NEVER LET GO I II III
By Robert Baptiste
NEW TO THE GAME I II III
MONEY, MURDER & MEMORIES I II III
By **Malik D. Rice**
LIFE OF A SAVAGE I II III IV
A GANGSTA'S QUR'AN I II III IV

Jamel Mitchell

For the Love of Blood

By Ca$h & Rashia Wilson
THE STREETS WILL NEVER CLOSE I II III
By K'ajji
CREAM I II III
THE STREETS WILL TALK
By Yolanda Moore
NIGHTMARES OF A HUSTLA I II III
BLOOD AND GAMES
By King Dream
CONCRETE KILLA I II III
VICIOUS LOYALTY I II III
By Kingpen
HARD AND RUTHLESS I II
MOB TOWN 251
THE BILLIONAIRE BENTLEYS I II III
REAL G'S MOVE IN SILENCE
By Von Diesel
GHOST MOB
Stilloan Robinson
MOB TIES I II III IV V VI
SOUL OF A HUSTLER, HEART OF A KILLER I II III
GORILLAZ IN THE TRENCHES I II III
By SayNoMore
BODYMORE MURDERLAND I II III
THE BIRTH OF A GANGSTER I II
By Delmont Player
FOR THE LOVE OF A BOSS
By C. D. Blue
MOBBED UP I II III IV
THE BRICK MAN I II III IV V

THE COCAINE PRINCESS I II III IV V VI VII VIII IX
SUPER GREMLIN
By King Rio
KILLA KOUNTY I II III IV
By Khufu
MONEY GAME I II
By Smoove Dolla
A GANGSTA'S KARMA I II III
By FLAME
KING OF THE TRENCHES I II III
by **GHOST & TRANAY ADAMS**
QUEEN OF THE ZOO I II
By **Black Migo**
GRIMEY WAYS I II III
By Ray Vinci
XMAS WITH AN ATL SHOOTER
By Ca$h & Destiny Skai
KING KILLA
By Vincent "Vitto" Holloway
BETRAYAL OF A THUG I II
By Fre$h
THE MURDER QUEENS I II III
By Michael Gallon
TREAL LOVE
By Le'Monica Jackson
FOR THE LOVE OF BLOOD I II III
By Jamel Mitchell
HOOD CONSIGLIERE I II
By Keese
PROTÉGÉ OF A LEGEND I II III

LOVE IN THE TRENCHES
By Corey Robinson
BORN IN THE GRAVE I II III
By Self Made Tay
MOAN IN MY MOUTH
By XTASY
TORN BETWEEN A GANGSTER AND A GENTLEMAN
By J-BLUNT & Miss Kim
LOYALTY IS EVERYTHING I II
Molotti
HERE TODAY GONE TOMORROW
By Fly Rock
PILLOW PRINCESS
By S. Hawkins
NAÏVE TO THE STREETS
WOMEN LIE MEN LIE I II III
GIRLS FALL LIKE DOMINOS
STACK BEFORE YOU SPURLGE
FIFTY SHADES OF SNOW I II III
By A. Roy Milligan
SALUTE MY SAVAGERY
By Fumiya Payne

BOOKS BY LDP'S CEO, CA$H

TRUST IN NO MAN

TRUST IN NO MAN 2

TRUST IN NO MAN 3

BONDED BY BLOOD

SHORTY GOT A THUG

THUGS CRY

THUGS CRY 2

THUGS CRY 3

TRUST NO BITCH

TRUST NO BITCH 2

TRUST NO BITCH 3

TIL MY CASKET DROPS

RESTRAINING ORDER

RESTRAINING ORDER 2

IN LOVE WITH A CONVICT

LIFE OF A HOOD STAR

XMAS WITH AN ATL SHOOTER

For the Love of Blood